BEACH WALK

An Emerald Isle, NC Christmas Novella

by Grace Greene

Whatever the season ~ it's always a good
time for a love story and a trip to the beach.

BEACH WALK
A Christmas Novella

by
Grace Greene

Emerald Isle, NC Stories

Kersey Creek Books
P.O. Box 6054
Ashland, VA 23005

Beach Walk
Copyright © 2015 Grace Greene
Emerald Isle, NC Stories (Series Name)
All rights reserved.

Cover Design by Grace Greene

Print Release: October 2015
ISBN-13: 978-0-9968756-1-5
Digital Release: October 2015
ISBN-13: 978-0-9968756-0-8
Large Print Release: November 2017
ISBN-13: 978-0-9996180-3-5

AUTHOR'S NOTE

BEACH WALK takes place in Emerald Isle, NC. It is written as a single title (or standalone) but is part of the Emerald Isle, NC series. If you enjoy it and decide to read the rest of the series, start with BEACH RENTAL.

It's always a good time for a love story and a trip to the beach.

ACKNOWLEDGEMENT

My love and sincere appreciation to my husband, family and friends for their encouragement and support. Home wouldn't be home without you.

Books by Grace Greene

Stories of heart and hope ~ from the Outer Banks to the Blue Ridge

Emerald Isle, NC Stories
Love. Suspense. Inspiration.

BEACH RENTAL (Emerald Isle novel #1)
BEACH WINDS (Emerald Isle novel #2)
BEACH WEDDING (Emerald Isle novel #3)
BEACH TOWEL (short story)
BEACH WALK (A Christmas novella)
BEACH CHRISTMAS (A Christmas novella)
CLAIR: BEACH BRIDES SERIES (novella)

Virginia Country Roads Novels
Love. Mystery. Suspense.

KINCAID'S HOPE
A STRANGER IN WYNNEDOWER
CUB CREEK (Cub Creek series #1)
LEAVING CUB CREEK (Cub Creek series #2)

Single Titles from Lake Union Publishing

THE HAPPINESS IN BETWEEN
THE MEMORY OF BUTTERFLIES

www.gracegreene.com

BEACH WALK

One house. Two people in need.

One winter night, a young runaway, Kelli, stumbled onto the porch of an oceanfront cottage. The woman who lived there, Margie, took her in and gave her the gifts of safety and security.

Twelve years later, Margie dies. Kelli continues living at the cottage until the day the woman's nephew arrives for a Christmas visit and intends to stay.

Dylan has been on the road for many years. He calls himself a traveler, but he's tired of always being on the move. When he arrives at his aunt's home, he learns that she has died.

Who has the better claim? And how far will Kelli go to keep the house that has become her home?

BEACH WALK

Chapter One

In the early morning the beach belonged to Kelli and the local wildlife. Walkers were rare at this hour, especially late in the off-season. The view from Margie's front porch, beyond the dunes and the grasses, stretched across the ocean to the horizon. To the left was the sunrise, to the right was the sunset, and in-between there was no one in sight. Even the footprints left in the sand the day before were erased overnight. Kelli owned this world—if only for a little while.

She leaned against the porch rail and nibbled on a slice of buttered toast. Crumbs fell on the front of her sweat jacket. She brushed them off. No one cared how she looked. If anyone was out here at this hour, they wouldn't care. The sand pipers and sea birds flew the same whether or not Kelli washed her face or brushed her curly brown hair. Her overalls were old and her sweat jacket, worn over her washed-out t-shirt, was huge. Margie had gotten both the jacket and t-shirt for her from a thrift bag at a nearby church. They were comfy and soft. Her overalls were cut-offs, so the morning air felt brisk against her bare skin. It was chilly, being early December, but not too cold to enjoy a walk along the ocean, and Kelli couldn't stand the feel of heavy wet denim flapping around her legs like chains. With the sweat jacket on, she was warm enough up top. When the sun rose the rest of her body parts would warm up, too.

Kelli's life was good. All good. Except for losing Margie.

The tide was going out. She crossed over the dunes via the wooden walkway and kicked off her sandals before descending the steps to the sand. She trudged barefoot through the dry mounds to the damp, smooth sand for easier walking.

She looked back to the west, toward Ron's place. He wasn't out yet. Not surprising given his age and the morning chill. She'd catch him later. He and Margie had been friends forever. Kelli had questions and he was her best and only legal source.

At the sunrise end of the beach strand, camouflaged in this dim, misty pre-dawn, an early walker was out, after all. Kelli's heart jumped to a quicker beat as she watched him. He stared at the ground, hardly moving. Her reaction was reflex even after all these years. This guy was harmless, probably hunting for shells. Some folks wanted to be first. To see it first. To get it first. To get a jump on the other guy. She could tell by his silhouette and by the way he moved that he wasn't a kid, nor old. Men on the beach at this hour were usually jogging or fishing which was probably why he caught her attention. If he was shelling, then he was at the wrong place. People around here knew Emerald Isle was a great place to live and vacation and the beach was the best, but for shelling, Shackleford Banks was the destination—a world-class shelling beach where the wild horses ran. So this guy was just someone passing through.

The walker, never more than a dark, distant figure, turned right, toward the houses. He disappeared into the misty fog down by Betty Threatt's house. Once again, Kelli was alone.

In warmer weather, she'd be surf fishing, not walking. Ron, too. She and Margie, in front of their house. Ron in front of his own. Something about the tug on the line, the thin fiberglass rod and reel dipping and pulling, focused her. Kelli worked the line and loved it.

She and the elements. Yet with a sense of negotiation with nature—one woman versus the elements. The meal at the end was a plus, but when money was tight, as it usually was, it was also a gift.

By the time the sun was clear of the horizon she was walking back to the house. It was time to shower and get ready for work. She had the early shift today. It was her turn to greet the lunch customers. She'd wear her crisp blue shirt and name badge and her best smile. Kelli was happy to do it because she loved living here and there was nowhere else she'd rather be.

~*~

More than a decade before Kelli had stumbled up onto Margie's porch, a half-starved teenager, a wanderer, to curl up for the night. Looking at herself now, fixing her hair and putting on a bit of makeup, that bedraggled, worn-out girl was nothing more than a faint, sad memory.

Sixteen and passing for eighteen, she'd seen this house, small and plain, with no lights burning. Summer was in the past and many of the houses were vacant, but dark windows could deceive. The bigger, fancier houses seemed riskier, too, as if their owners might value them more and thus keep better watch. This small house was tucked between them and set a little way back. Almost unnoticeable. Kelli had stood on the wooden crossover eyeing the dunes and the beach in both directions, and saw no one. It was off-season, November, so no wonder. Still cautious, she walked casually and quietly toward the porch and the house.

Kelli broke rules. She had to if she wanted to survive on her own, on the streets. But she didn't think of herself as a criminal, not then or now. At this small house, the curtains were closed. No light was visible. No noise. Not even a faint TV hum. She paused with her hands on the windows. She did a quick push up against the frame in case the window was unlocked. No movement. She tried the door knob, but it didn't turn.

This wasn't a fancy house, the kind owned by someone with deep pockets. Damage, and the cost to repair it, might be a problem. Doing damage wasn't Kelli's style.

She pulled an old plastic poncho from her backpack, wrapped it around her body and curled up in the most protected spot, in the right-angle where floor met wall. With the legs and rungs of the Carolina rocker between her and the porch rails, she felt almost invisible to anyone passing by. From down on the beach, no one could see her, or mind that she was here. She wanted to fall asleep to the sound and smell of the Atlantic. For the past year, she'd never passed the same way twice, so it was important to pay attention to where you were at any given moment because tomorrow was...well, it was tomorrow and who knew what that would bring?

That night the moon glowed. It hung over the foaming waves and lit up the dark. The sky filled with stars by ones and twos, and then by bunches. None of those balls of fire and gas shared its heat with her. The seasons were changing, and it was time to move farther south. But that night, she lay on her side, the poncho wrapped close around her and with her legs pulled up to make a smaller target for the chill, and she thought how lucky she was to have oceanfront accommodations. And that she was alone. This wasn't the city. There was no one in the vicinity to disturb her or cause her harm. If she hadn't been hungry, this would almost be a real vacation.

Kelli's alarm clock would be the sun. When the first light touched her eyelids, she'd be up and on her way. No muss. No fuss. She traveled light and when she felt safe, she slept well.

But before the sun rose that morning, the porch steps creaked, and the floor boards shifted as someone came to stand near her, watching her as she slept.

~*~

In the darkness, Kelli dreamed the porch was a raft, floating and pulling loose from its moorings—the house. The dream was a wisp, a moment of half-waking, before she sensed someone nearby and rose swiftly to her knees, her back pressed against the wall, her hands extended palms forward with the fingers curling into claws, ready to fight or run.

A small, dark-haired woman stood a few feet away. Her features and expression were difficult to make out in the pre-dawn light. Kelli relaxed a bit. Not only small, but she was older, too. Unless the woman had a weapon hidden or some sort of superpower, she could get past her without difficulty. Kelli's claws turned into fists as she rose to her feet.

The woman touched her forehead, appearing puzzled. "I thought someone's tarp had blown onto my porch?"

It was a stupid statement, not a real question, but full of puzzlement and wonder.

Kelli sensed no fight here. This woman knew nothing of fists and violence. Kelli could simply leave. Ignore her. Walk past her before she thought of calling the cops. If the woman screamed, Kelli could vanish into the semi-darkness in a heartbeat. She grabbed up her backpack to do exactly that and the woman's hand shot out.

"You're cold. Hungry." The woman saw Kelli's face and pulled her hand back. "Breakfast," she said. "Let me fix you something to eat."

Kelli looked around seeking the trap and saw none.

The sky was lightening though the sun had not yet breached the horizon. A pile of dark objects was silhouetted on the sand just beyond the porch. A fishing pole was the only recognizable item, and maybe a folded lawn chair.

"Come inside. Warm up and have something to eat before you move on. My name is Margie. This is my house."

Kelli had nowhere special to be. No actual destination. If she'd had a better option, ocean or not, she wouldn't have spent the night on those hard, damp planks. This woman, Margie, invited her inside for breakfast and she went. Because…why not?

Margie Manning fed her a hot breakfast. Under her gentle insistence, Kelli moved from the breakfast table to the laundry room. After all, who would it hurt if her clothes got a good washing? Kelli sat in Margie's robe, fresh from a shower, and Margie said, "Let's go find some shoes that will fit decent." Kelli needed better shoes, so she thought, "Why not?"

Kelli had intended to spend one night on the porch before moving southward. Instead, she spent the next night on Margie's sofa. Then Margie fixed her a spot in the spare room. Kelli waited for the inevitable questions. That would be her sign to slip out of town. The questions didn't come. After a while Kelli found ways to be helpful, to show she wasn't a beggar or a mooch. She made sure to greet her hostess each morning with a smile, and each night Kelli wished her a good night's rest and sweet dreams. Margie offered good food, solid and comfortable shelter, and no particular worry over money. Margie was alone in the world, too, with a couple of longtime friends for company, but no one else.

Kelli didn't have much, but she was smart. Feeling welcomed, and glad of the roof and a real mattress, she wanted to please.

Margie was short, average in features and not much for style, but she did have a superpower. Margie Manning possessed kindness and innocence, cloaked in love. Kelli accepted her invitation for breakfast and stayed twelve years.

~*~

When Margie got sick, and knew how sick she was, she said, "I don't want you to worry over me. You've put your life on hold. You deserve better."

"That's stupid," Kelli said, pretending not to know what Margie meant. "I've had a boyfriend or two. You know what Betty says—better none than the wrong one."

"The day comes when pat phrases don't serve. When they aren't enough. You're almost thirty. Still young, but time–"

Kelli picked up the half-empty water glass. "More ice water? Or juice?"

"Just water. Nice way to change the subject, by the way. Don't think I didn't notice."

In the kitchen, Kelli added water and ice over a slice of lemon. She put a sugar cookie on a plate. Margie's favorite. Maybe she'd enjoy the cookie and let the subject of boyfriends drop. The guys Kelli had met were nice enough, but one day the light would hit them right, or wrong, literally, and their shadowed faces would remind her of men who'd lived in the alleys and underpasses in her prior life, and she couldn't get away from them fast enough. She'd tried to tell Margie, to explain it, but there was a limit to what...to the unpleasantness Kelli wanted to share with her friend. Margie's heart and spirit were gentle. When it came to romance, Kelli decided long ago that she'd take a pass on it.

She set the plate on the nightstand and straightened the blanket over Margie's legs.

"Thanks, honey." Margie continued their conversation. "I married, you know. It didn't last long and I didn't have children, but I did have that one adventure. Love and romance. You're young yet. Act like it. Don't pretend you're past caring. One day, you'll wake up and realize you waited too long."

"If love and romance want to find me, I'll be here waiting."

"Smart-aleck."

"Seriously, I'm happy, Margie."

"So am I," she answered. "You're the daughter I never had."

Less than a month later Margie died.

She made it to Thanksgiving. No turkey, stuffing and gravy that year. Kelli sat on the side of Margie's bed and held her hand. The flesh was cool, too cool. With her free hand,

Kelli smoothed Margie's hair back from her face. As her last breath was spent, the warmth of it touched Kelli's arm. Margie passed with a soft sigh. No drama. Only a gentle departure. That's who she was.

After a few minutes Kelli eased off of the side of the bed. She moved as if it might still be possible to disturb her friend. She closed the front door softly behind her and walked up the beach to Ron's house.

Kelli knocked on the door. He opened it and saw her face. The creases deepened around his eyes and he drew in a quick breath. He said, "She's gone."

Ron made the calls.

As the mortuary took Margie's body for cremation, Ron would've followed them out, but Kelli stopped him. She tugged on his sleeve and asked, "How long before I have to get out of the house?"

He blinked.

"You know I'm not hard or heartless, Ron. I wish she was still here, but she's not and I have to figure out what my life looks like tomorrow and after."

Ron said, "What do you mean? I know she wanted you to have her place. Did she give you her will?"

"No." Kelli sighed.

"You didn't ask her? You knew she was going."

She shook her head. "I couldn't. We thought she'd make it to Christmas. We thought she still had time."

"I assumed...." He touched her shoulder. "Sorry, Kelli. Margie gave me the money and the legal docs for her funeral arrangements years ago after her sister died. I kept them safe for her, but that's it." He perked up. "I know she made another will. I saw her do it. You've got to find it." He scratched his cheek, thinking aloud. "Sam Barrett was an old friend of hers. A lawyer. He might have given her some advice about it, or held it for her or something, but he died last year. I could ask around. Meanwhile, you've got to search the house and find it."

Ron left and she went to Margie's room. She started to tidy the bed. She should wash the sheets, she thought, but then, instead, she sat on the coverlet and curled into a ball hugging Margie's pillow.

Almost thirty. Kelli had a job as a hostess at a restaurant, a relatively fancy one at a hotel, but not something she could support herself with. She had depended upon Margie. She had Margie's house to come home to each day—Margie's house and Margie's stretch of beach and ocean. In season, they fished on the beach early and late, and in winter Margie made little googley-eyed shell creatures that the gift shops stocked to sell to the tourists come spring. Kelli had laughed at them, but she also named them and talked to them like they could hear her, and had made Margie laugh.

Kelli didn't fit in with the world outside of this house and its beach, and that was the truth.

Ron had managed the cremation as Margie directed, and now, less than two weeks later, the shell creatures still sat where she'd last worked on them. The finished ones were lined up on the shelves of the bookcase, while the books were stacked in corners. Dust and sand, a hazard of the beach, had covered the shells and collected around them. Dusty sand. Sandy dust. It could stay there for all Kelli cared, at least for now. No doubt the dust bunnies were having a party beneath the beds and dressers. Maybe later she'd care. Right now, no.

She washed the few supper dishes and dried them. She'd never done much cooking and had done even less since Margie passed. She went out to sit on the porch steps and watched some lonely sea gulls scanning the beach for scraps. The pickings were lean this time of year.

She'd stay here in Margie's house until they, whoever *they* might be, kicked her out.

Ron walked up the beach and angled through the soft sand toward the house. He was barefoot and his legs, below the ragged hem of his worn shorts, were scrawny and tanned. His face was equally skinny, as well as stubbly with a few days growth of beard.

"Hey, there, Kelli. Fine evening."

"It is."

"Maybe winter has decided not to visit this year."

"I wouldn't count on it."

"You work today?"

"Sure did."

"You doing okay, then?"

"I am." She looked away, wanting to erase the sorrow from her face before she looked back at him. Ron and Margie had been friends for decades. His grief was no less, and maybe more, than hers.

"I was thinking about what you said."

Kelli asked, "Said about what?"

"About staying. If you could find the will that would solve the problem."

"It will solve it only if Margie left me the house. Even then, I might not be able to cover the upkeep and the taxes and all."

"She wanted you to have it, to live here."

"No luck with the lawyer?"

"No, sorry. I know he had a daughter in the area. She might know where his papers went if she's still around, but I have to find out her name before I can figure out where she is."

"Thanks for trying. I've looked for the will. I've been through almost everything. I haven't been able to go through her clothing and personal stuff yet."

"You have to make yourself do it. Sooner or later taxes or insurance or a leaky roof are gonna raise their ugly heads and you'll run into problems."

"I believe you. I've tried, but I'll try harder."

He slogged away through the sand toward the sunset end of the island. He lived three houses up. Like Margie's, his was a tiny house sandwiched between the bigger, fancier rentals. Their small houses were almost invisible. They sat quietly anonymous in the midst of the coral, turquoise and sea green vacation homes.

Kelli knew there were things like taxes and such. There was no mortgage, so until taxes were due, she didn't think anyone would worry about the property too much. Maybe not even then, for a while. Evictions took time. By then, she'd find the will or figure something out.

~*~

Her car was old but reliable. It had taken Kelli to her job at the hotel restaurant for six years, and had carried her and Margie to the doctor when she started feeling bad. Not fancy and rather dull, but reasonable and reliable.

Customers were light today with only a mild crunch at lunch. They needed fewer waitresses this time of year, so despite being the hostess, she filled in and helped where needed. As the afternoon ran down the manager asked if she'd like to leave early. She needed the pay and the hours, but the opportunity to get home before dark this time of year, to maybe read on the porch or something, was irresistible.

As usual, she parked behind the house and entered through the back door. She dropped her bag on the kitchen chair, then went to the living room to grab her book. The curtains were open. Margie liked them open and so did she. Margie didn't tolerate blinds or shades. Nothing was welcome to come between her and the sunlight.

Through the wide front window, Kelli saw a dark figure down on the beach. She paused for a closer look.

A man. He stood by the stairs down by the

end of her crossover. Distant. Plus, he was facing the ocean, so it was hard to see details. When he started walking Kelli released her breath. She'd been holding it and hadn't realized.

He was moving on. He'd just been passing by. But something jiggled in her memory and nagged at her. She decided not to sit outside, after all. Instead, feeling restless now, she cleaned the kitchen and threw in some laundry to wash. A short time later, she returned to the window. He was standing on the crossover now. Kelli stayed at the window to watch him.

The stranger wore jeans and a jacket. His hair was longish and dark brown, maybe black. From the back, it was hard to tell his age, but she guessed he was maybe thirty-something. He moved like he was in shape with no slouch in his posture or stance. Very thin.

He turned to face the house and stared as if he could see right in through the window to where she stood. He couldn't—not from that distance, she knew that—but she stepped back anyway, shivered and hugged herself.

Things were different since losing Margie, but a new sort of normal had been re-sorting itself. Now, seeing this dark-haired stranger on the crossover, Kelli knew nothing would ever be the same at Margie's house, certainly not for her.

She backed away from the window and turned slowly to face the bookcase. It was full of books, shell creatures and loose shells, but Margie had arranged a few framed photos on one shelf. Kelli reached up and took down a gold frame. The photo was of Margie's sister. They looked a lot like each other. In front of the sister, sat her son, Margie's nephew. Kelli brushed the dust from the frame and glass as she took it over to the window. The kid in the photo was no more than ten. The man on the crossover was twenty years older. But the hair, the bone structure in his face, the tilt of his head—the resemblance was unmistakable. What was his name? Margie had talked about him a lot in those first years. He hadn't been to visit in all the time Kelli had lived here. To her knowledge, he hadn't even contacted his aunt. If he had, Margie would've been so delighted she'd have spoken of it.

Kelli gripped the frame so tightly her fingers hurt. He hadn't been here in ages, hadn't been in touch. Now, a mere two weeks after her death, here he was, steps away from her front door. Kelli didn't believe in coincidence. She did believe in fate, and its mindless, careless cruelty.

He was here, the unworthy nephew. He hadn't come when Margie could've enjoyed his visit. Not even in time for the small funeral. But, as her one living relative, he was here for her estate—the house and whatever went with it.

The cold pit in Kelli's stomach expanded. It reached into her chest and arms, causing her head to ache. It had taken so long for her to be 'at home,' to believe she had a home, that she could be at home anywhere. A decade hadn't been long enough. Only a lifetime of safety would convince her that she was secure.

Don't get ahead of things. Hearing Margie's voice in her head soothed her. Don't assume, Margie would say. Don't borrow trouble.

Kelli breathed slowly and deeply to reduce her heart rate and to warm that iceberg lump inside. After a last look at the photograph, she placed the frame face down in a drawer, not back on the shelf. She slid the drawer closed, and waited.

The knock on the door never came. When she looked back outside, he was gone.

It didn't feel like trouble gone, but more like trouble postponed.

~*~

Yesterday seemed distant. The man on the crossover was a wisp of memory, mostly. Kelli was determined to keep him in the mist until he vanished altogether. She grabbed her tote bag and locked the back door as she left. The day was a fine one, with a high blue sky and fresh ocean breezes. A light jacket was enough. The restaurant was only a few miles down the road and in the off-season, an easy drive. When you threw in the tourists, you never knew how long it would take to drive the distance, but without them, there wouldn't be much need for the restaurant, so she always smiled when she greeted them as they entered the restaurant and escorted them to their tables. She smiled and she meant it.

Menus. One each for the party of four in the corner table in section two. The rolled-up silverware was already on the table waiting for them.

Kelli nodded as they sat. "Your server will be here in a moment to take your drink order."

She headed back to her position near the entrance. Lucy paused as she passed and said, "My parents are so excited we're coming for Christmas. Thanks for picking up some of my hours. Mr. Beale wouldn't have agreed to give me the days off if you weren't covering for me."

"No problem." Kelli nodded. "Happy to help." Truly, she didn't mind. The holidays weren't special to her. Never had been. Not with the home life she'd had. That first Christmas with Margie, when Kelli realized how much it meant to her, she'd made an effort for Margie's sake. And every year thereafter. But on her own? For just her? Why bother?

After closing Kelli pitched in with the waitresses to roll the silverware and fill the condiment containers. Nadia was chatting about her boyfriend and Lucy went on about her little girl. Kelli nodded and said the right things, but didn't contribute. She spoke Margie's language, not theirs. She lived Margie's life, not that of a twenty-something. They didn't understand. Kelli was so different from them. At times she sensed they might feel a little threatened by the difference. Yet they knew so little about her. What would they think if they knew the rest of the story? She didn't think their opinions would improve.

As they walked out into the night, Nadia and Lucy veered to the left side of the parking lot. Kelli's car was parked at the far end. The moon was bright and this island was her home, or an extension of it, and she was never afraid of night on the beach. With enough light to see by when she needed it—usually supplied by the moon and stars—she had no worries.

Back home, she walked into the living room and flipped on the light switch. She stopped dead. The curtains were open with a view of the black night beyond, and of a man's pale face and two large hands pressed against the glass.

Chapter Two

Kelli flew to the door. Frantic, she ran her hands over the knob lock and the deadbolt, making sure they were bolted and secure, then she threw herself against the door as if that might help support it against invasion. As she pressed against the door, she heard a man's voice.

"Hello?" he said again.

Her heart hammered. The beats pounded in her ears.

In a stronger voice, he called out, "I'm sorry I scared you." After a pause, he asked, "Are you there? Is anyone there?"

The curtains. They were still wide open. Kelli left the door and fell across the sofa in her haste to drag the curtains closed.

"Hey, it's okay. I'm just looking for my Aunt Margie. Margie Manning? This is her house, right?"

She returned to the door, her brain spinning. She sagged against it.

Him. It was him.

"My name is Dylan. She might have mentioned me?"

Kelli yelled through the door, "I'm calling

the police. Go away."

"Okay. Okay, just listen. Can you answer my question? Is my aunt at home?"

Aunt. So she was right. And she wasn't happy about it.

A relative. A blood relative. But if he'd come to visit his Aunt Margie, then he didn't know she'd died. Unless he was lying, pretending not to know. Blood didn't always count for much, except in a court of law. And to police, probably.

"You can't spy on people. You're a peeping tom. It's against the law." She paused for a breath. "I've called them. The cops are on the way. You better go fast, now while you can."

"How long before the cops get here, do you think? I'm guessing they're locals. Would you let them know I'm not armed? I don't want to get shot in the dark while I'm waiting."

Was he calling her bluff? Mocking her?

"Leave and you won't have a problem."

Pained groans and muttering, sounds of frustration, came from the other side of the door. There was a thud, maybe caused by a shoe hitting the porch plank or maybe it was a fist against the wall, followed by a muffled ouch.

He said, "I don't have a car. No way for me to go anywhere. Look, I thought I'd find my aunt here and spend some time with her. Visit her for the holidays. I wasn't expecting...."

Her. Kelli. He wasn't expecting her.

She yelled at the door. "I wasn't expecting you either, and you need to leave. Go away."

After a long pause, he asked, "Just tell me one thing? Is this my aunt's house? I'm sure I remember. I used to visit her when I was a kid. This has to be the right house."

He sounded so weary. But there was no place for him here.

"This is her house. She isn't home."

Another long pause. Kelli waited.

Finally, he spoke. "I'll hang out on the porch until the police come or Aunt Margie gets back."

He sounded defeated. She stepped away from the door, undecided. His voice in the dark, and outside on a cold night, brought back her own memories of feeling lost, alone and with no future. Without even a present worth enduring.

She'd lived differently for the past decade and she wouldn't give it up easily. "You're going to have a long wait. I don't know when she'll be back."

He said nothing.

"She's...she's visiting friends." Kelli struggled. "If you'd called first...."

"Yeah." He spoke slowly. "Look, I don't have anywhere to go, not tonight. And no way to get there if I did. Can you give her a call? She'll tell you who I am. You can ask her if it's okay to let me inside." His voice trailed off. When she didn't respond, he said, "Okay. I get it. Not happening. No worries, I'll sleep on the porch. I won't bother you, I promise. If my aunt isn't here in the morning, I'll go away. I'll leave. Guaranteed."

A grown man with no place to go and no way to get there? "It'll be cold tonight with the onshore wind. Go to a hotel."

"I'll be okay."

His words were spoken so softly they barely make it through the door, but she did hear them and her heart was moved.

Kelli shook her head, no, but the words pushed past her lips anyway. "I'll throw out a sleeping bag. That's the best I can do."

"Deal."

"I hope I'm not making a mistake."

"If I'd known she wasn't home I wouldn't have bothered you tonight."

"How could you?" She spit the words out.

"What?"

Kelli shouted through the door. "Know she isn't home, of course. How could you know? She hasn't heard from you in...how many years? More than ten, I know that much."

She sensed, more than heard, the increased pressure of his hand against the door. Instinctively, she placed her own over where his must be.

His tone changed to sullen and resentful. "You don't know me or anything about me. It's easy for you to criticize because you aren't looking me in the face."

"You're the one who showed up unannounced after so many years. Do you blame me?"

"For what? For judging me?"

"No, for keeping the door shut between us."

He said, "Keeping... Yes. No. I mean I can't blame you for that. You don't know me."

"Exactly."

"What I mean is, don't blame me for not being around. You don't know anything about my life." The tone of his voice changed back to the calm, thoughtful tone. "Look, I'm sorry."

"I'll be right back."

She pulled the sleeping bag down from Margie's closet. Margie had used it like an extra quilt on cold, windy nights. Kelli pressed her nose to it. It smelled dusty. Nothing she could do about it. In fact, if he minded, he could do without and was welcome to move on altogether. She passed through the kitchen on the way back to the living room and grabbed a few more items.

At the front door again, she yelled, "Move back." She waited and heard no answer. "Don't try anything."

"Promise."

His voice seemed to have shifted and she was pretty sure he'd moved down the porch. She eased the deadbolt open, then twisted the knob lock. In one fluid movement, she yanked open the door and tossed the sleeping bag out. The water bottle escaped the folds of the sleeping bag, landed hard with a plastic thud, and rolled across the boards.

In the few seconds the door was open, the night air rushed in bringing the salty cold of the ocean with it. Not a gale or anything, but just a soft, steady breeze. She slammed the door shut and flipped the deadbolt back into place.

"Thank you," he called out. After a few moments, he said, "Water. And what's this?"

"The cookies? Just something in case you're hungry."

She waited for him to say thank you again, but this time there was no answer.

"Remember, you try anything at all—rattle a door knob or even breathe near the door—I dial 9-1-1. They'll be here fast. You're lucky I didn't actually call them before. In the morning,

I expect you to leave. Go away. Early. I'll tell Margie you were here when she gets back."

"Yeah."

"Okay. Good night."

Kelli waited, but he didn't respond. She peeked around the edge of the closed curtains and her last view was that of his face, pale in the night, holding Margie's sleeping bag.

How could she possibly sleep? It wasn't guilt. After all, what choice did she have? As it was, he was fine and snug in Margie's sleeping bag under the shelter of the porch and with the ocean singing a lullaby. And here she was—lying in bed, warm and cozy, but unable to relax because a strange man was camped outside the front door, with what intentions? If he left as promised, then his intent wouldn't matter.

Kelli got up to peek through the curtains a couple of times, but could hardly see anything. Finally, she did sleep and awoke just before dawn.

~*~

Remembering, she rose to her knees abruptly. The bed swayed and the mattress creaked, but otherwise, nothing. The bedroom door was closed. There was no present danger. She grabbed her robe and tiptoed down the hallway and to the living room. She listened, then carefully moved a curtain aside for a look.

In the pre-dawn light, she could make out part of the sleeping bag. A shoe was abandoned on the porch. Dylan was rolled up next to the house, close to the wall, just the way she'd done so many years earlier.

The curtain dropped back into place.

She sat on the sofa. She had to tell him Margie had died. Margie was his aunt. It was the right thing to do. She'd take him a hot cup of coffee, tell him, and then he'd go.

Kelli pulled on her jeans and a clean T-shirt, washed her face and brushed her hair. By then the coffee was ready. He might be gone by the time she got outside and that would be totally okay with her. Before going out, she shrugged into her sweat jacket.

Juggling two mugs, sugar and sweetener packets, and creams, Kelli unlocked and opened the front door. She set it all on a small table Margie and she had used for coffee on sunny mornings when they weren't fishing. Despite the commotion, he didn't move, so she closed the door again, this time with force.

The bag stirred like a shifting landscape. His dark hair became visible at the far end.

She'd expected the aroma of the coffee would draw him out, but with his head inside the bag it couldn't work. She coughed and cleared her throat. No good. She went right up to the bag and nudged it with her foot. The bag stirred again. A low groan came from it.

Most of his head emerged from the sleeping bag. He looked confused. "It's not morning," he grumbled. "It's the middle of the night."

"The sun is rising and the coffee is cooling." She held up a cup in salute.

He looked at her, then half-turned to peer beyond the porch rails. He stared at the dark ocean beneath the lightening sky, then ran his fingers in his hair. "You're kidding, right?"

"Do you take cream and sugar?"

He scowled. His dark brows came together. The crazy, disordered hair and the stubble on his cheeks and chin gave him a scruffy look. This wasn't some kid. It occurred to her that perhaps she should be more cautious, but it wasn't dark—she was out here in the awakening daylight—and rightly so or not, for now, she had the upper hand. Her biggest interest was to get him up and out and away.

"No." He eased upright.

His backpack lay nearby, by no means stuffed full. Only the one shoe was in sight on the porch, but he'd slept in his jeans and t-shirt.

He kicked out of the sleeping bag and rose to his feet. He was several inches taller than she. Kelli put on her official hostess smile and held out the cup of coffee. "For you."

He scratched his jaw and ignored the offered coffee mug. He was still navigating the warp jump from sleep to the present. Oddly, lamely, he said, "Thanks for the cookies and water last night."

"I'm glad they were useful."

He snagged the free shoe and dropped it beside the table. He was still wearing the other shoe. As he sat, the chair creaked. He eyed it, gave it a wobble and apparently decided it wouldn't collapse beneath him. He pulled the stray shoe onto his foot and looked up at her.

"Your coffee is getting cold." She took a deep breath, then said, "I have some news...bad news. I should've told you last night, but last night was so strange."

He picked up the mug and folded his hands around it. He sipped the coffee, then closed his eyes as he emptied it. When he sat the mug on the table, drained, he said, "First off, I don't know your name."

"Kelli."

He nodded. "Nice to meet you, Kelli.

Thanks for the coffee."

"You're welcome." She shrugged. "I'm sorry. I don't know a better way to say it than to just say it. Your Aunt Margie passed at Thanksgiving. She got sick. Pretty sudden. I would've let you know if there'd been any way, any thought to…but even if I'd tried, I wouldn't have had any idea of where and how to find you."

His mouth opened, then closed. He looked down at his feet. "I just missed seeing her." He looked back up at her. "You live here with Aunt Margie? Lived, I mean."

"Yes. For a long time." One quick intake of breath, then the exhale, and she added, "She gave me the house and her stuff. I'm sorry you came all this way for nothing."

"Not nothing." He shook his head. "I had oceanfront accommodations. People pay big bucks for that. Plus, the amenities of bottled water and cookies." He gave her a crooked smile.

When he smiled, he lost some of the scruffy pirate look. Humor gave his face, his eyes, an intriguing light. When he smiled, it seemed as if she was catching a glimpse of the real person, but his eyes looked sad.

Her heart did a little flip. She was going to make an offer she might regret, but this wasn't about her. This was about Margie. She owed Margie, and Margie would want Kelli to be kind to her nephew.

"I could scramble you an egg or something. Toast, if you like. Before you go."

He didn't respond. He was staring past her shoulder with an unreadable look on his face. She looked and saw the window trim. The old painted trim was flaked and peeling. She'd known it wasn't perfect, of course, but when you lived with something, day in and day out, you tended to accept its state as part of its character. This morning, it looked shoddy and uncared for.

"That would be great."

Kelli looked back. He was staring at her now. Not really staring, but looking friendly. She tucked a stray hair behind her ear. She regretted the offer already, but couldn't think of any way to take it back without seeming ridiculous.

She opened the door and waited. As he grabbed his pack and the sleeping bag, she forced herself not to slam the door in his face. Instead, she pointed and said, "The bathroom is that way."

Keep it simple, she told herself. She was a poor cook at best. Eggs, toast and juice. She could manage that much without making anyone sick.

The shower ran forever, or so it seemed. He must be using every drop of hot water in the tank. She stared at the bathroom door, remembering. She wouldn't begrudge him one hot shower. She decided to wait for the water to stop before heating the pan for the eggs.

Kelli sat in the kitchen, trying not to overthink it. He was in the bathroom longer than she expected, even after the water shut off. Was he going through the medicine cabinet? Margie's fixtures were old and her bathroom still had a shallow metal cabinet with a swinging mirrored door. Not very interesting.

Unless he was thinking about the bathroom and cabinet as his.

It seemed clear he hadn't come to claim Margie's stuff because he hadn't known she was gone, but it didn't mean he wasn't going to try now that he knew.

He wandered out, no guilt on his face. "It looks just like I remember it."

Margie's words came to mind and popped out of her mouth. "It's old but it all works. Not a thing wrong with any of it. Your aunt wasn't one to throw something out just because it was old or out of style."

His dark eyes lit briefly. With a tease in his voice, he said, "No, ma'am."

"Have a seat. The eggs will be done in a few minutes."

He shoveled the eggs into his mouth as if he hadn't eaten in a while. The eggs were gone before he ever touched the juice and the toast.

The silence felt awkward.

"Where do you live now? Where do you go from here?"

He paused mid-bite. "Undetermined."

"Would you like another slice of toast? More juice?"

"If you don't mind."

"No problem."

Kelli turned her back and took a minute to rearrange the expression on her face. She could handle giving him a second piece of toast and juice, but that was it. It was time for him to be showing signs of hitting the road. The Margie voice inside of her, instilled by a decade of living with that wonderful woman, versus the fresh-from-the-streets Kelli who had suddenly returned from the past with a vengeance, were struggling for dominance— kindness versus survival. If he didn't leave soon, Kelli was afraid of who would win, or who might get hurt.

"You said she was sick?"

Margie. He was asking about her death.

She put the toast on his plate.

"Sick. Her heart. She went within a few weeks of finding out there was a problem."

He nodded. "That's how my mother went, too. Long time ago now." He looked thoughtful. "Maybe it runs in the family." He shrugged. "Well, no one will care. I'm the last." He pushed a sad smile across his face.

"Your mom was a lot younger, right? Might not have been the same thing at all."

"It's okay. Don't worry about it. So, you took care of everything? The funeral and all that?"

She sat down again. She shrugged. "Me and an old friend of hers. A neighbor. It wasn't much. Margie didn't want a lot of fuss."

"Where's she buried?"

"Buried?" What to say? "On the bookcase. The urn."

"Oh."

His vacant look came and went pretty swiftly. He stood and walked over to the bookcase. The urn was on the shelf surrounded by Margie's shell creations. The shell creatures, the shell encrusted picture frames, even a series of shell ballerinas and princesses on top of little music boxes. Dylan reached up and touched them. He pulled his hand away and rubbed his fingers.

"It's all dusty. I haven't moved anything. It's

just as she left it, except for the urn, of course."

"What about the house? Her stuff? Oh, that's right. You said she gave you the house. I could give you a hand with some fix-up around here. Looks like neither of you did much of that."

"No, thanks. I can handle what needs doing."

"Sure." He turned back toward the bookcase. "It'd be cheap. Just room and board maybe? A place to stay for a couple of weeks?"

Despite his casual attitude, she recognized begging when she heard it. She steeled herself. "It won't work."

"I'll sleep on the porch."

"I don't know you." Kelli put the dishes in the sink and used that as an excuse to hide her face again. She ran the water, refusing to turn around. She let it run over her fingers as it warmed and the suds grew. "No offense. I'm sorry, but no. It's impossible."

"I understand. Guess I'll be on my way."

Those were the words she'd been anxious to hear. But she couldn't keep Margie's voice at bay in her head. "If you need a job, I could ask at work. See if someone knows of any hiring around here. We always need kitchen crew at the restaurant during tourist season.

Not so much this time of year, but I'm happy to ask."

"No, thanks."

Well, if he was too good for that kind of work then there was nothing more she could do for him.

"Okay." She turned around. "Good luck on the road."

He picked up his backpack, dusty from travel. The strap he put over his shoulder was faded and fraying. He smiled, nodded and said, "It looks like a great day for a walk."

Guilt again. "I could drop you off somewhere. Save you a few steps. You'll have a better chance of picking up a ride along the main road."

He shook his head, still smiling. "No, I prefer walking. A beach walk doesn't sound half bad." He nodded and exited, closing the door behind him. Kelli was left standing there holding the dish towel.

It was all good, right? She walked over to the bookcase and touched the same shell creatures Dylan had touched. She rested her fingers against the cold metal urn.

"I hope I didn't treat your nephew too badly. I fed him. I loaned him your sleeping bag. Practically five-star accommodations." She wanted to laugh at her wit, but it fell short of funny. "Margie. I'm sorry, but I can't invite in a stray man I've never met. Not possible and not smart."

It was her day off. She double-checked the door locks, then went to shower and dress. She gave Dylan credit—he'd left the bathroom neat.

He'd be okay. Obviously, he knew how to take care of himself. Meanwhile, she had some errands to run. If the weather held, she might actually make it out to the beach this time.

Kelli kept an eye on the time as she went from the drug store to the post office to the grocery. An hour gone. Almost two hours. By now, Dylan should be well out of the area. She went home, scanned the beach and saw no one but an elderly couple out for a walk and a couple of kids trying to get a kite up in the air. She grabbed her lawn chair and went down to the wet sand. She stretched her legs out, put the open book over her face, and soaked up vitamin D while the salt breezes wafted around her. The curling fringes of the waves rushed up the sand to wash her toes. She missed fishing. Her next day off, if the weather was reasonable, she'd pull the bucket and pole out of the shed and have some fun. Not much fish this time of year, so fun was all it was likely to yield.

When the sun began to drop and the air picked up a chill, Kelli carried her chair up to the porch and went inside. She took the fresh filets she'd picked up at the grocery store to cook them on the small smoker Margie and she sometimes used on the front porch. Of course, once on the front porch, she thought of Dylan. Was he hungry? Had he found a place for the night?

Not her business. Not her problem.

She could've spared him some fish, though. She wrapped up the leftovers, did the cleanup, and popped a movie in the VCR, one of their many favorites. Margie had favored Star Trek and Jane Austen. Kelli didn't really get the connection. Margie said it was all about possibilities. This was Jane Eyre, one of Kelli's personal favorites. All in all, it was a nearly perfect day. But in the silence of the evening, she missed Margie. No movie or novel could fill that void. Only time could work that magic.

~*~

The new morning was fresh and promising, and the ocean called. Kelli stepped out to the porch. Barefoot and shivering in her cut-off overalls, her hair tied back in a ponytail and her face unwashed, she was as content as anyone had a right to be.

A noise. She jumped. A body was on the porch, pressed up against the house. Appeared to be sleeping. No blanket. Only some extra clothing covering his face and chest. An old backpack was over his legs. He had to be freezing. She was angry. He was trespassing. He was determined to make himself her problem.

She intended to nudge the bag with her foot, but it came off as more of a kick.

"Hey!" He moved swiftly, rolling over and half-rising before seeing her.

"You're lucky I'm not wearing boots. What are you doing here? You left!" She shouted. She pulled it back a notch. On quiet mornings like this sound traveled. She didn't want to draw attention. "Why are you still here? Trespassing, that's what you're doing."

Kelli took a step back as he sat up. His hair was askew. His stubble was worse. "You look awful," she said, then cringed at her harsh tone. "Well, you do," she finished.

"I didn't hurt anything. I didn't bother you. I would've been gone before you knew I was here, but you are out so crazy early."

"Who are you to judge what I do, or when, in the morning? You said you were leaving.

You walked up the beach. You were gone."

"I wasn't bothering you or anyone."

"On my porch? All night? It's an invasion of my privacy."

He rubbed his hand over his face. "Why are you out here in the dark?"

"It's not dark and it's none of your business what I do at dawn. None at all."

"Of course not. Didn't say it was."

Now what? She slapped the sides of her thighs then put her fists on her hips. "If you aren't going to leave, I'll have to call the police. You're forcing me to do it. I'm sorry, but I can't have you hanging around like this."

Dylan rose to his feet. "Hanging around? I came to visit my aunt, got here and found you instead. I'm happy to leave, to move on, but with no money and no car, it's not so easy."

Kelli crossed her arms. "But you're too good to take on kitchen work."

He looked away, beyond her, to the horizon. "It's not that simple."

"Turn on water? Make suds? Et cetera..." She made handwashing motions.

He sat in the other chair. "No official work history, no fixed address, no money, no transportation. It's like money. You can't get money unless you have it already. It's a lot harder to get a job if you don't have one."

"There might be some truth in that, but mostly it's just excuses. You can't move forward unless you're moving forward. You can't get up the ladder until you put one foot on the rung and then the next, one step at a time."

"Yeah. And where will I live while I'm earning those bucks? Will they let me sleep in a storeroom? Or how about the alley behind the place?"

He yanked up his drooping socks. His hands were shaking. From the cold, Kelli was sure. One of Dylan's shoe laces was broken and knotted halfway up. He straightened his shirt and jacket, then grabbed for his backpack. He headed off the porch.

"Hey, I'm sorry for the … lecture…pep talk…whatever it was."

He paused and looked back. "Don't feel sorry for me. I travel by choice. Mostly on foot because that's what I like. I don't need much and I do what I want to do and when. I'm only sorry I missed seeing Aunt Margie." He shook his head. "Fact is, I have a friend with a car who's coming this way in a week or two. He's going to swing off the highway to pick me up. We're headed to Florida. Maybe New Orleans. I'm just hanging out until he shows up. Almost anywhere will do."

His dark tousled hair looked a lot like Margie's when she came in fresh from a windy morning of fishing. His brown eyes had that soulful look of hers, too.

"Let's take a step back, okay? No promises, but maybe together we can think of something over breakfast."

"Breakfast again? You sure? I can manage on my own."

"On my porch? That's managing?" The words came out her mouth like an accusation, a disparaging one, and sounded like someone she didn't know, didn't want to know. "About breakfast, I'm sure. For the rest, there's bound to be somewhere in town where you can crash for a few days. Just not here. Or maybe your friend can pick you up sooner?"

He followed her inside. She pulled the oatmeal container and the box of raisins from the cabinet. While Dylan was in the bathroom, she heated the water and poured in the oats. She struggled to find the emotional balance between common sense and kindness. When he rejoined her in the kitchen, she still wasn't sure, but there was no point in being wishy-washy. As he sat at the table, she said, "I leave for work at ten a.m. I can ask around there about shelters and stuff, if you want, but I'm not comfortable with you being here, especially while I'm gone."

"Oatmeal. I haven't had oatmeal in…I don't know how long. Sugar?"

"It's already got sugar in it." But she set the sugar bowl on the table next to him anyway.

"Do you have more raisins?"

He was halfway through the bowl of oatmeal, with lots of sugar and milk and the extra raisins he'd added, when he asked, "Is the porch off-limits?"

"Are you kidding me?"

He shrugged. "I don't want to make you angry again. Or disrespect you. I appreciate the food and the use of the facilities." He nodded toward the bathroom. "I'd like to repay you. If you have some tools, like maybe a scraper, I can work on the porch and those window sills. Get it prepped for painting."

At least he'd be busy.

"Out in the shed. I can unlock it for you. It's junky, but whatever tools we have are in there."

"Deal." He grinned. "Weather's nice. Great day to work outside. Mind if I do some laundry?"

She stared.

"Don't get worked up, Kelli. I can put the wash in now and then toss it in the dryer when you get back home."

Work outside? Laundry? He sounded so pleased about it…and clearly intended to still be here when she returned home after work. She left him there, but outside as they'd agreed. She recognized something in Dylan she'd felt in herself long ago. The joy of simple uncomplicated tasks when surrounded by chaos and uncertainty. It wasn't something she wanted to relive, but she wasn't blind and the common trauma was easy to see.

At work she stayed busy engaging with the customers, and was driving home when the doubts re-emerged. She'd brought extra home from the restaurant. Pretty good eating, actually. The cook, when he'd packed it up and she'd asked for extra, said he was pleased her appetite was returning.

"You're a sweetheart, Georgie." She picked up the bag. "Actually, I have a guest for a short time. She'll enjoy this as much as I will."

She. How could Kelli say he? Georgie would make assumptions and boyfriend talk and speculation about her personal life would be all over the restaurant. No, thanks.

Her heartrate increased. In anticipation, not dread. It was kind of fun to be going home to someone. But also dangerous. After supper, could she send him back out to the porch?

Oh, yeah. No question. She'd do what she

had to—whatever was necessary to keep her status quo intact.

~*~

Kelli entered through the back door, set the food containers on the table, and then continued to the living room. First, she looked out the window. Dylan's shoes were visible. He must be rocked back in the chair. She unlocked the door and stepped out to the porch. His eyes were closed. Napping? The curling paint from the window sill was gone. Gone from the railing, too. It was scraped right down to the wood. She needed to buy paint. What kind? She had no idea. Most of these houses had vinyl siding and trim. But that was way out of Margie's budget and hers.

Dylan opened his eyes and asked, "What smells so good?"

She nodded toward the door. "Supper." She took a second look at him. Despite the dark stubble there was something.... "You look different."

"How?"

"I don't know. Relaxed?" Less tension around his eyes, maybe? They seemed less shadowed.

He nodded. "It's a good day."

"Good. Let's eat before the food gets colder."

"I'm invited? I'll be right there." He stood, adding, "As soon as I put the clothes into the dryer."

The dryer door shut as Kelli put the napkins and flatware next to the plates. Dylan wasted no time. He was in the kitchen before she'd opened all the food containers.

"Help yourself. I have to take these containers back tomorrow so don't toss them."

Dylan was already spooning the stroganoff onto his plate.

"I can heat it up for you?"

"No, thanks. Still warm." He pointed his fork and dug in.

Two hungry people sitting at the kitchen table sharing a meal—Kelli knew there should be conversation, even if they were strangers. Maybe like the tidbits ladies and gentlemen exchanged in those Jane Austen movies when they were dancing. Clever little impersonal tidbits with everyone being very polite and nodding at each other until it was time to leave. In this case, Dylan was focused on the food and nothing else.

And when it was time for Dylan to leave? What then? He was eating so fast, it was going to be soon.

As the last bite cleared his plate, before he'd finished chewing and swallowing, he was up and gathering the dishes. With a quick twist of the faucet, he had the water running in the sink.

Kelli said, "Don't worry about it. I'll clean the kitchen."

He shook his head, no. "I've got this."

Without ifs and buts, hems and haws, as soon as the dishes were done, he asked for the sleeping bag. "You don't mind, do you?"

She looked toward the porch, feeling guilt and relief. He hadn't put her on the spot. She was grateful. "Nope."

"One thing."

"What?"

He nodded toward the books, books in the bookcase, books stacked in the corner, books on the end table. "Mind if I take one with me?"

"How will you read in the dark?"

"Flashlight."

"Oh." She shrugged. "Well, why don't you sit in here and read for a while…before you go out for…" She stumbled over the end of the sentence. He wasn't an animal to be put out for the night.

"Sure you're okay with that?"

"It was my suggestion, so yes." She pointed toward the television. "I'd offer to turn the TV on but we aren't hooked up to cable or satellite. Margie and I have a collection of videotapes."

"Videotapes? As in VCR?" He half-smiled, but then picked a book. He chose a thick volume about the history of England.

It was one of Margie's thrift shop acquisitions. Same place they picked up used videotapes. But she kept that thought to herself.

"Are you into history?" she asked?

"I'm interested in lots of things, history among them."

Kelli set her jaw and pressed her lips together. She wasn't going to make any smart remarks about his choice.

Really, who was she to judge? She picked up her own novel and settled in the corner chair. She was re-reading an oldie, but goodie, *A Devil on Horseback* by Victoria Holt. One of Margie's favorites. She'd called it a comfort read. Reading it, knowing Margie could almost have recited it by heart, made her feel close. But tonight, Kelli had trouble focusing. She kept wanting to ask Dylan where he'd been and why? And did he know how hurt and worried his aunt had been? And so on. But each time, the words died before being said. She didn't want to open that door. Encourage the relationship. Give him ideas. And it wasn't just her. She sensed the wall he'd put between them despite the cozy picture they presented.

He focused intently on the pages before him. Kelli wasn't convinced he was actually reading. She kept glancing at him. Once he caught her looking and smiled. She stopped checking.

After a while, her eyelids grew heavy. She could almost imagine Margie was back and curled up on the sofa, flipping the pages of her book. Any minute now Margie would say, "Kelli, you sleepy head. Go to bed and get a good night's rest."

Margie didn't, and Kelli couldn't decide how best to tell Dylan it was bedtime, and time for him to leave. At some point, Kelli dozed off. She woke much later with a sense of time having passed. The curtains were closed and only a kitchen light burned.

Dylan was gone. His book had been left neatly closed, with a bookmark in it, on the coffee table.

~*~

Kelli left by way of the back door and walked through the sand between the houses. Her front porch had a temporary occupant and she didn't want to disturb him.

Away from the house, it was almost like old times. Pre-Dylan. She walked farther than usual. Way past Betty Threatt's house and the others that were so familiar. She walked until her feet were almost numb from the cold wet sand and wavelets. By the time she turned back, the sun was well up and so was Dylan. He was sitting at the top of the stairs to the crossover.

She stopped a few steps below where he sat. She blurted out, "Where have you been all these years? You should've kept in touch with Margie."

He leaned forward, resting his arms on his knees, kneading his fingers. Then he stopped abruptly, separating his hands, holding them palms up. "What did Aunt Margie tell you?"

"That you spent summers with her when you were a kid. Your mom died and you lived with your father and she never heard anything from you again. She called and sent letters, but your dad returned them, and finally they came back undelivered with no forwarding address."

"Yeah, my dad. My parents were divorced. When Mom died, I moved in with my father. It was a disaster. Always. That's how he lived his life. He stayed out late, drank too much. He never paid a bill he could put off. We lived in a constant state of emergency. I had a counselor once, who called it that. She said some people have it like an addiction, you know? Living in chaos. They like dancing on the edge of a cliff. Sounded almost like a poem. I remembered those words. Threw them at my dad once and got backhanded. He didn't see the poetry. Or didn't appreciate it, anyway."

"We lived in Florida, moved to Arizona. Never stayed anywhere long. I got into trouble. One day we just parted ways. I've been on the move for a long time."

"But..."

"But what?"

"Well, you're no kid. If that's what you've been doing since you were a teenager, it's a wonder you're still alive. You don't have a drug habit, right? Because I can't deal with that. I'm not a doctor or a social worker or a cop."

"Hey, calm down. The answer is no."

"But you lived on the street? Because that's how it sounds."

"I'm a traveler. A loner. Unencumbered. Nobody's victim."

"I'm glad to hear it."

"Why?"

"Because you're Margie's nephew. I

wouldn't want her to be disappointed."

"I don't think she cares now."

Kelli ignored that. She stepped up onto the bottom step, her hand gripping the wooden railing. "So what's changed?"

"What?"

"Well, you were a solitary wanderer, now you're sleeping on the porch and eating my pitiful cooking. Why'd you come looking for your aunt after all these years?"

"I don't know. I always thought I would." He shrugged. "By the time I was on my own, I didn't feel like that kid she'd known, been kind to."

She knew what he meant. He couldn't go back without erasing the sweet, loving, all-good-things-are-possible memories of him Margie held in her head.

"I'll yell when it's time for breakfast." She started walking up the crossover toward the house.

"Hey," he called after her. "So I passed?"

"Passed what?"

"All those questions... Wasn't that some kind of test?"

"Not so fast. We'll call it undecided for now." She paused at the door. "You can use the bathroom and shower or whatever, if you want."

They repeated the routine for several days. Except for the meals and the bathroom, he stayed outside. He stayed busy, probably to keep busy. Each night he went out to the porch as if it were a matter of course. Kelli couldn't decide whether it was sensible, or just bizarre, but for now, it had to serve.

Both Ron and Betty stopped by. Betty asked, her cane making dents in the porch floor, "You know you got someone sleeping on your porch at night?"

"I do."

Ron said, "I told her it was okay, that it was Margie's nephew and you had it handled."

Kelli asked, "How'd you know he's Margie's nephew?"

"He paid me a visit during the day while you were at work. I remember him from when he was a kid."

"That so?" Small town. Emerald Isle was really only a small town for the locals.

He added, "I put him to work doing a couple of odd jobs I hadn't gotten around to."

"Here, too. You can see he scraped down the sills and rails. I have to get some paint."

"Don't bother," he said.

"What? Why?"

"Wrong time of year to paint. He'll have to wait until warm weather returns."

Lovely. Sounded like she'd be the one finishing the job.

A puff of wind blew a curl from Betty's carefully sprayed gray hair. She pushed it out of her face. Ron was holding her arm to steady her. Kelli asked, "Would you like to come in?"

Betty said, "No, thanks. Margie's gone. Seemed like checking on you was my duty, but I don't want to see for a fact she's not here. Easier to pretend she's still with us that way."

Illogic. But nothing Kelli could argue with.

"I'm fine, Miss Betty. You and Ron don't need to worry. I'm not a kid, you know."

"Which makes it all the more of concern, my dear."

Ron helped her down the stairs. Her thin hair in a tight bun, and wearing a dress and sweater, but her feet were bare, the better to negotiate the sand. They could've come by the road and to the back door. But they didn't. They were beach people. Kelli smiled. So was she.

~*~

Kelli swung through the kitchen after her arrival at work.

Georgie called out, "Good morning, Kelli. Hey, you hear about the weather? Big change coming."

She smiled and waved. "It's just weather. Nothing to get worked up over."

The smile was for show. It was December and moving rapidly toward Christmas. A change in the weather was inevitable. It was also inconvenient.

A regular customer sat at his usual table. She brought his coffee over.

"Good morning, Kelli. Maybe good afternoon?" He laughed and checked his watch. "Did you hear about the weather? Hope you've already got your Christmas shopping done. Stay in out of the cold."

"No worries. It's all handled. Merry Christmas, Roger."

Christmas. No shopping this year. Not for gifts or special treats. The one gift she'd bought, the box for Margie to decorate, was it.

It was a busy lunch shift and everyone who came into the restaurant mentioned the weather. Wind and rain were expected. The front was rolling in that evening. Hello, winter. She was uneasy, but not due to the weather. Rather, the easy companionship, the polite arrangement she and Dylan had managed, felt threatened.

Chapter Three

She pulled up the short driveway to the house. Indecision knotted her insides.

Inside the house, all was silent as it should be. Kelli went out to the porch looking for Dylan. The strand stretched generously in both directions. Only a few people were out. Dylan was nowhere in sight.

Had his friend arrived early? She didn't see the backpack out here.

She didn't believe he'd gone. Not without saying goodbye unless he'd had no choice. No, he was out on the beach somewhere. Walking, walking, and walking, if she could believe him. But not in the morning. He wasn't a morning person.

She leaned against the porch rail, amused. The beach belonged to her in the morning. For the rest of the day, to Dylan. Funny.

As she turned, she noticed a piece of driftwood propped up against the wall. A fair-sized piece. Its twisting branches, smooth and gray, wrapped around each other and pointed this way and that. Kelli picked it up and ran her fingers along the smooth, almost glossy surface. Sculpture-like. She returned it to where Dylan had left it and went inside.

Margie's room. Kelli had tidied her bed, straightening the spread and fluffing the pillows, but otherwise nothing had changed, except for the thicker layer of dust and fine sand. It found its way in no matter how tight the house. And the truth was, Margie's house wasn't tight. Dylan had been right when he noted they hadn't been into upkeep. They didn't have the skills and Margie couldn't afford the repairmen, but a house on the ocean, blasted by sand and salt, must have upkeep, regular and expensive, or it would fall apart. She felt a moment of defeat. Even if she could keep the house, how would she afford the work that needed doing?

The curtains were threadbare. Margie's clothing was still in the drawers. Her Christmas gift to Kelli, the decorated box, still sat above the dresser on a wall shelf, wrapped around and around in red ribbon. Margie put it there in plain sight to tease her. Kelli had refused to touch it, pretending she hadn't seen it, for the purpose of teasing Margie. They could get a lot of amusement out of little things.

Margie was still here.

Kelly moved down the hallway to the room at the back. It wasn't much more than a closet and opened into the laundry room and mud room. If she cleared the boxes and other junk out there was room for a cot. Margie had a cot somewhere. Not great accommodations, but it would certainly beat huddling on the porch when the cold rain blew in off the ocean.

"Hello?"

"I'm here. Come on back." She walked into the kitchen.

He stopped at the invisible line between kitchen and living room. "You look like you have something on your mind."

Kelli leaned back against the counter and crossed her arms. "I do. The weather is going to turn tonight. I don't know what to do about it."

He laughed. "What are you? Mother Nature? You aren't responsible for the weather."

"Not what I meant. I was thinking about the porch."

Some of his good spirits subsided, but he regained his cool. "Don't worry about it."

"There's a room in the back. It's small."

The sudden silence was profound. She thought, help me out here, Dylan.

He pulled a chair away from the table. Her chair. "Sit down. Did you have anything planned for supper?" He waited. "No? Let me cook. I'm not half-bad." His voice had changed, softened.

"There was nothing to bring home today. I was going to stop at the grocery store, but I was distracted by the whole weather thing. I forgot."

He looked in the cupboards and the fridge. Soon, he was pulling stuff out onto the counter. Canned chicken. Butter. Milk. Pretty basic. Bread. He stared at it, then started banging the pots around. "Looks like white sauce with chicken over toast." He waited for input and when she didn't respond, he moved ahead.

Dylan looked comfortable at the kitchen counter. He used the manual can opener and flipped the chunk chicken can over to drain into the sink. He found the measuring cups as if they, and his fingers, were magnetized.

"What do you want to do?" Kelli asked.

He twisted to glance at her. "Are you asking if I want to sleep in the rain?" Then he put his attention back to measuring out the cornstarch and the milk. "No. Can't say I do, but I can see you're still uncomfortable with me in the house. It's okay."

"I appreciate what you've done around here, though Ron said it's the wrong time of year to paint outside. Guess you didn't know." She cleared her throat. "I wish I could say I was comfortable with…you know."

"Consider me a boarder? Could you do that?"

He heated the milk, stirring it as the butter melted and the cornstarch thickened. When the consistency of the white sauce was right, he dumped the chicken in to heat. He popped the bread down in the toaster.

"How'd you come to be here, living here, with my aunt?" he asked as he put plates on the table.

Deep breath. She shrugged, releasing the growing tension in her neck and shoulders. "I needed a home and she offered. She was very kind. We did well together."

"And she gave you her house. I'm glad."

Kelli felt a tiny bit dishonest. Margie had told her the house was hers, but without the legal documents she felt unofficial, not legal and definitely insecure. She couldn't tell him. In fact, he was being less than honest, himself. As Margie's only relation, he'd expected to jump back into Margie's life and be there to inherit when the time came. He might've said he liked to wander, but if that had been true at some point, she didn't think it was true any longer.

Plates. Utensils. Napkins. He delivered the toast to each plate, and put the pot of white sauce and chicken on a hot pad on the table. He offered Kelli the ladle with a flourish.

"More. Put more on. There's plenty."

It was a lumpy gravy-like white blob. Many blobs. Covering her toast. She tried to smile as she tasted it. It was hot. "This is good. Better than good."

He smiled. "Hey, don't act so surprised."

"Good at paint scraping and a good cook, too."

"I have many talents." He dedicated himself to eating. When he was done, he said, "You still don't trust me. You can, you know."

"You're a psychic, too?"

"I can read expressions. Have to be good at reading people when you live like I do."

Was he hinting he'd read the deception in her face? About the house?

"Where do you go during the day?"

"I walk a lot. I like to walk on the beach."

"That's your story?" she asked, half-joking.

"My story and I'm sticking to it."

Kelli settled back in her chair. She was determined to push the awkwardness away. "Ron says you've been a help to him." She tried to appear casual. "Supper was delicious. I'll get the dishes done and then we can pull the boxes out of the back room."

As she stood, he jumped up saying, "I've

got it."

Suddenly she didn't know what to do with her hands. They were just there in the air, suspended mid-grab for the pot. She pulled them back, touching her hair and clasping them. "I'll go ahead and get started in the back, then." She gave an awkward chuckle, still unsettled, pre-empted. "I have to go through the stuff anyway. Might as well start now. Some of Margie's creations are in one of those boxes. I promised a gallery in Beaufort the last of her stock."

"Gallery?" He was running the dish water.

"Yep. She's got quite a trade. Did have, rather."

In the end, he washed and she dried. It seemed a more natural course. Less artificial. And it only took about five minutes from start to finish. Not much of a mess, really.

Dylan unstacked the boxes in the corner. The word, Christmas, was scrawled in big faded letters on one of them. He pulled up a flap. "I remember this stuff. Looks like the same silver tree she had when I was a kid."

It was. Was he mocking Margie? Her tree? "Just put it over there."

He cast a quick look at her. "Whatever."

In the end they cleared out the back room, mostly by moving the boxes into other rooms.

Kelli found the cot in Margie's closet and set it up.

"Here are the sheets. I'll get a pillow and blankets." The uneasiness was back and she avoided his eyes.

"Well, okay then."

He looked back, moved toward her and touched her arm. "You can trust me."

"Sure." She shrugged, and stepped back. They, she, needed more space between them.

That night was awkward. In fact, after a while she gave up trying to play it cool and pushed the dresser in front of her bedroom door. It squeaked on the wooden floor. Did he hear it and know what she was up to? Good. Let him be warned that she was prepared. She was nobody's fool.

~*~

Kelli awoke to the smell of coffee brewing. She stretched, then remembered. She started up and almost reached her knees, before she fell back onto the coverlet and pillows. The dresser was still in front of the door and she'd had a great night's sleep. Whatever might have happened outside her door hadn't bothered her one bit.

She dressed then moved the dresser, as

softly and quietly as she could, and went to wash up. She brushed her hair, trying to smooth some civility into it. So curly. And so long since the last trim by Margie and her scissors. Kelli leaned over the sink to look more closely in the mirror. More freckles. Some faint lines near her eyes. Another between her eyes. Well, it was to be expected. She wasn't a kid and she spent a lot of time outside.

Her t-shirt was the usual. She tugged at it, assessing it. It failed to please.

Back in her room, she looked through her clothing for something that looked less disreputable, but then realized what she was doing. What was good enough yesterday and the day before, was good enough today. Nothing had changed overnight. Nothing important. She slammed the drawer shut. She was fine as she was. And she'd be fine after he was gone. She kept on the soft, well-worn jeans, but as a concession to being a hostess in her own home, she put on a regular shirt. Nothing fancy, but it did have buttons.

Delicious smells greeted her as she entered the kitchen. Dylan called out, "Good morning. Hope you're hungry."

Kelli sat at the table, content to be waited upon, marveling. "If you've been on the road for the last few years, how did you learn to cook?"

He shrugged. "Just always have."

Dylan was like a different person. One night under a proper roof. Free access to a normal bathroom and kitchen, and he was practically glowing and he moved with easy assurance. He needed a haircut and a shave badly.

Not her business.

He grinned. He'd moved in. Not just physically, but also emotionally. *Mistake, mistake, mistake*—the words echoed in her head.

"I've got some odd jobs lined up so I'll be gone for part of the day."

Off-season at the beach was prime time for repairs. He might have something good going here, but Kelli kept her mouth shut. Did they really know who he was? In people's homes. In her home. He was Margie's nephew, but he'd been living rough for a long time. He was a stranger. A man might have a pretty…well, not pretty, but intriguing face, but that was just a mask that men wore and you could never be sure what moved behind it.

Well, one mistake often led to another. Kelli said, "There's a spare front door key in the bottom drawer of the end table."

He looked aside, staring at nothing, then

coughed lightly before saying, "Are you sure?"

It was an uncomfortable moment, and no need for it, really.

"Of course. It's necessary. What will the neighbors say if I leave you outside to freeze on the porch?"

~*~

Blustery, but the sky was blue and the fluffy clouds were high and white, so the day looked more pleasant than it felt.

Kelli was excited. At work that afternoon, the cook and the manager had been exchanging sharp words. Georgie was saying his assistant was going to be out for a few days. Mr. Beale said, "Why is it always this way this time of year? Holidays and summer. Why?" Georgie started to speak, but Mr. Beale waved him down. "No, I know the answer. Don't like it though." Georgie said, "For good help, sometimes you have to make allowances."

She stepped forward. "Sorry to interrupt. I know someone who can cook. He's just passing through but might like to pick up a few hours of work, if you're interested."

"Short term and part time," Mr. Beale said. "If that sounds good to him, have him come in and see me."

She could hardly wait to tell Dylan. This was his chance to earn some cash, more than an odd job or two. He could ride with her. She was going that way anyway, right? True, he had a friend coming to pick him up sooner or later, or so he said. A job would help him earn a little money which might help him move on.

Kelli entered through the back door. "Dylan?"

No answer. Nothing cooking in the kitchen. In fact, no signs of life.

She ran to his bedroom door—the closet room. His backpack was still in the corner. A shirt was hanging on the bedpost. She leaned against the door jamb. He was taking a walk or doing a job for a neighbor. She moved at a more casual pace into the kitchen to see if he had anything defrosting on the counter. Seriously, it hadn't taken long at all to grow accustomed to having a cook in-house. And a good cook.

Nothing on the counter.

She wanted to speak with Dylan about the job. She felt deflated, at loose ends until he chose to return. She wandered to the front window thinking she might step outside and check the beach. The wind was dying down, but still blustery, making the dry sand a nuisance, at times painful unless you like being sand-blasted.

Someone was down by the ocean, surf fishing. He moved awkwardly. The waves were rough and foaming. The rod seemed to be getting the best of him. In this surf, it was no wonder, really. Not the right conditions for fishing... Dylan.

Kelli pressed close to the glass. Where had he gotten the fishing gear? Margie's and hers, of course. Their equipment.

She blasted through the front door and stormed down the crossover. She didn't yell. She didn't want to distract him and risk the ocean swallowing the equipment.

As she flew across the sand, the dry grains kicked up by her feet and blown by the wind stung her legs. She went straight for the fishing rod, grabbing for it. Dylan was in motion, struggling with the pole and the drag of the ocean. As he turned, wrenching the line back from the greedy waves, his elbow made contact. With force. With her face.

She sprawled backward. Her head hit the soft sand, her cheek stinging.

Dylan reached for her, releasing the rod, his expression moved like quicksilver from anger to panic. "What were you doing coming up behind me like that? I didn't see you!"

"The rod!" She pointed as it slid across the mixed barrier between sand and water, pulled by the outgoing wave. "Grab it!"

He reached toward her again. She sprang up, pushing his arm aside, and threw herself at the fishing rod as it was being swallowed by the ocean. She grabbed at the line, her fingers scrabbling as the wet sand filtered over it, and she missed it. Suddenly, Dylan flew past her. He fell with a stumble and a belly flop. He grunted, but was immediately back on his feet. Both of them dashed into the waves, grabbing for the rod and nearly drowning each other.

Their motion stopped. The water continued to foam and stream around their knees, but Kelli's hands were empty. Dylan, however, held the rod in one hand, the end dangling in the water. He lifted his hand and only part of the rod was there.

"I guess we landed on it," he said.

Kelli looked at the broken piece of fiberglass and then out at the ocean.

"It's gone," he said. "I'm sorry."

She looked beyond him at the upturned bucket and the lawn chair on the beach, then back at his face.

"What?" he asked. "I said I was sorry. What's your problem? I found them in the shed."

"Not yours," she said. "That stuff isn't yours."

"Hey," he said, "it's just a fishing pole."

"A rod. A rod and reel, not a fishing pole. And it didn't belong to you."

His face turned a deep red and with a violent gesture, he threw the broken piece out to sea.

Kelli screamed at him over the ocean and through the wind, "It belonged to Margie!"

"I know," he yelled back. "I saw it and I remembered."

He turned and kicked at the water as he walked toward the chair. She could see by his body language that he wanted to kick the chair, maybe throw it. Her anger matched his and silently, she dared him to abuse the lawn chair, ready to pounce if he did.

He wrapped his fingers around the top rail of the chair but he didn't throw it. He took the chair in one hand, and the bucket in the other, and stalked across the dry sand to the side of the house. He disappeared from view.

~*~

He remembered fishing with Margie. So did Kelli.

Wet and cold, she dropped onto the sand

and stared out at the sea. She dug her wet, gritty fingers into her hair. Did one of them have a better right to the memory than the other?

"Hey, kiddo."

Ron. She looked up at him reluctantly.

"I'm almost thirty. I don't qualify as a kid anymore."

"Grumpy, then. A grumpy old lady."

"Thanks, Ron. You know how to cheer me up. Not."

"Is it him?"

Kelli looked up. "Him? What him? Dylan?"

"Yeah. Margie's nephew. He kind of reminds me of her. I dunno exactly. Eyes or hair? Something. But not his temper. He seems okay and then he doesn't. You having any trouble with him?"

Kelli didn't know what to say.

He waved his hands at the beach and houses behind them. "Everybody was talking about how he was sleeping on the porch, especially with it being almost winter. I have to say I wasn't too sure about what was best. Not about him moving inside either. I will say he's been helpful around the neighborhood."

"Has he?"

"Very handy. Makes himself useful." He shrugged. "More so when you were keeping him locked out of the house. Not as much now."

She smiled. "He's fine. He was fishing with Margie's gear and I over-reacted. I don't know why."

Ron eased himself down onto the sand beside her. "Sure you do."

"Yeah, I do. He was trespassing in my territory. My memories. I didn't think about what the memories meant to him. And, in the end, it's just a stupid fishing rod. Not even an expensive one. Irreplaceable, though. Margie made it last forever...well, for years anyway." She shook her head. "He had a rough life, Ron. I guess his best memories are from his childhood."

"No excuses, Kelli."

He was staring at her cheek. She touched it and it ached, but only a little.

"No, no excuses. For either of us. Including me." She added, "This was an accident."

"I saw the show."

"Yeah? Glad you found it amusing."

"I remember him as a kid. I was surprised he remembered me. When her sister died, Margie wanted Dylan here with her, but his father...well, it didn't work out."

Kelli nodded.

"He was a nice kid, as far as I recall, but

that doesn't change anything. When it's time for him to go, it's time. You don't owe him. You have to think of what's best for you first."

She nodded again. It was easier said than done. People owed in different ways for different things.

"Did you hear?" he asked.

"About what?"

"The Sullivan's. Their house."

"What about them?" The Sullivan's owned one of the fancier houses a short distance down the strand. They rented it out and used it themselves from time to time.

"Someone broke in."

"What? When?"

"A little over a week ago. Maybe two weeks. Hard to know."

About the time Dylan arrived. Kelli cleared her throat. "Theft? Or damage?"

"A little of both. Not too bad. But still…." He shrugged. "Beginning of the month. They don't know the exact day because they were out of town and it was unrented. When they got back, they discovered someone had been inside."

Beginning of the month. Dylan. No, of course not. "No others, right?"

"Not that I've heard of. Just wanted to remind you to lock your doors. You never know. And if you're ready to get rid of your guest before he's ready to go, you tell me. Margie's nephew or not, I don't cut him no slack."

"You aren't accusing Dylan, are you?" The warning note in her voice surprised them both. Ron shifted away ever so slightly.

"No, but now that you mention it, let me add one more thing. You can't save him. You can't fix him. Whatever his troubles are, regardless of why, it don't matter. Women do that. Margie did that."

Her back stiffened. "You mean me."

He frowned. "No. I mean her husband, and he broke her heart for her troubles. Did she ever tell you about him?"

Kelli shook her head. "Not much." She shivered and rubbed her sleeves. As her anger cooled, the wet clothing became colder and itchier.

"Women like to think they can fix men. It's the maternal heart, I guess. But in my experience, it doesn't work out well for either the guy or the gal."

He shifted to one hip and rose to his knee. "It's a longer way up than it used to be." He chuckled, and making it to his feet, he shuffled off through the sand. "Don't take on trouble, Kelli. You've had enough of your own and done well to overcome it. It doesn't mean you're able to take on someone else's." He pointed at her. "You need to get inside before you get sick. This is the wrong time of year to be frolicking in the ocean without a wet suit."

"Frolicking? Did you really say that? Is that what it looked like to you?"

He snickered. "Not precisely frolicking. You know what they say? A thin line between love and hate? Maybe there's a thin line between fighting and playing too. Just make sure you both know where the line is." He paused. "Do you have plans for Christmas?"

"Christmas?"

He shrugged. "Well, you know, with Margie gone this will be your first alone. Betty mentioned it. Said maybe you were worried about being alone for the holidays....because you know you won't be. Don't need to be. There's me and Betty and our other friends. You've always got us. If Dylan's still here, he can join us, too."

"Thank you, Ron." She bit her lip before she could say anything more.

"We're old. But we might do in a pinch. That said, if you get a better offer, don't worry about hurting our feelings. You're young and should be living a young life." Ron walked away. The sand covered his sandals, then flipped off of them with each step. He didn't look back.

Kelli closed her eyes and buried her face against her arms. Now what?

~*~

Her feet dragged, wet shoes and all, as she crossed back to the house. When she entered the front door, she stopped to listen. No sound, no indication Dylan had come inside.

Before stepping inside, she brushed as much of the sand off as she could. Her clothes were cold and clammy and she wanted badly to change, but first she had to speak to Dylan.

She went down the hall to the back door. Through the glass, she saw him sitting on the back steps. The shed door was closed.

Did she owe him an apology? It felt like she did. Maybe for over-reacting? Or maybe she didn't. He had permission to get tools out of the shed, not Margie's fishing equipment. Temptation—the kind from memories that twist in people's hearts—had they been too much for him? Did it excuse his actions? Probably not. But none of it excused her own.

Maybe she should ask him about the house that was broken into? No way to mention it without him thinking she was accusing him. Partly because she couldn't think of any way to say it without it being in the forefront of her mind. Did she think he had? She had no idea. Sometimes people broke rules, important rules, if their need was great. It wasn't always as simple as right and wrong. Sometimes it was just the way of the world.

~*~

Kelli opened the door. The hinges sighed, but Dylan didn't look around. He moved his head enough to show he was aware. She stepped out and moved cautiously forward unsure of herself and of him.

His back—his shoulders, his spine, the nape of his neck—the damp t-shirt clung to his torso. His black hair was disordered and wet around the edges. A shiver rolled down the muscles in his back. Her hand reached forward of its own accord and, stunned by the instinctive reaction, she yanked it back.

"Go ahead," he said.

She gasped, horrified that he'd somehow recognized the turmoil inside of her, turmoil she hadn't understood until now. Then, still behind him, she watched him open his hands and hold them palms up. He continued looking forward as he said, "Say it. Tell me what you want me to do. I don't know how I can make it right."

A deep breath and reality reasserted itself. They weren't friends. In fact, they hardly knew each other, but he was Margie's nephew and deserved better from her. She moved forward, touched the handrail and eased down to sit beside him. Slow and easy. Nothing sudden. He wasn't a wild animal that might feel threatened by a sudden movement—or was he? He flinched, moving slightly away as her arm brushed his.

"It wasn't yours," she said. "But it was only a fishing rod and I over-reacted."

"A rod and reel. I remember. She taught me all about hooks and lures. I think she was mostly afraid I'd catch myself instead of fish." He looked at the street as if it were an ocean scene twenty years past. "I saw the rod in the shed and...."

His voice trailed off. Kelli let the silence settle over them. It was strangely comforting. The chemistry seemed to have shifted. In a nice way. A cozy way.

From the corner of her eye she thought she saw a smile, small but still a smile, appear on his face. Her heart answered with a warm little blip.

He frowned, suddenly looking at her. "You okay?"

She followed his gaze and saw her hand

pressed over her heart. "I'm fine. Hungry, but fine."

Dylan rose and held out his hand. She accepted it and rose to her feet. "Thank you, sir."

"My pleasure. Did you get any groceries?"

She followed him inside amazed how a day could flip on its head several times in a row like an acrobat somersaulting across the floor.

"I think that's a 'no'? How about pancakes?"

"Perfect. Margie and I used to have breakfast for supper sometimes."

"First, I'm going to change and so should you."

She touched her shirt, her slacks. Yes, still wet. Somehow she'd lost that chilly feeling. Now it was just itchy.

"Good idea."

Still aglow, from what precisely she wasn't sure, she took his lead as they each went to change.

While Dylan cooked supper, Kelli retrieved the box of shell creatures from the back room and set it on the coffee table. There was enough room in the top of the box to add more. She gathered some from the bookcase, blowing at the dust as she picked them up. She grabbed several from the top of Margie's dresser. She paused, touching the ballerina shell jewelry boxes. There were only a few of those and they were her favorites. She wasn't ready to part with them.

Dylan came down the short hallway. "Supper's ready. Come and get it while it's hot." He came closer. "What are you doing?"

She looked up. "Remember the gallery I mentioned? The one in Beaufort? I need to run these up there tomorrow morning. Want to go along?"

~*~

In the morning, they drove across the sound via the bridge at Atlantic Beach and then again, over the bridge from Morehead City to Beaufort. Kelli turned down the narrow road by the cemetery and then turned again on Front Street.

Dylan didn't have much to say. He was focused on the scenery and whatever else went on in his brain. She was having a few doubts herself and left him mostly to his own thoughts.

Christmas decorations were up along the street and on the store fronts. The Front Street Gallery had a wreath on the door and the large plate glass window was framed in twinkling lights.

Kelli held the door open as Dylan carried the box across the threshold. The bell tinkled overhead. He stopped just inside the door and did a quick scan around the room, at the furnishings and artwork, and stopped when his eyes hit the service counter behind which a woman stood.

She looked up and smiled brightly. "Kelli!"

"Hi, Maia."

The woman, Maia, rushed from behind the counter and headed straight toward them. Dylan stepped aside and she threw her arms around Kelli in a quick hug, then ushered her into the gallery. The door swung closed with another tinkle. The two women paused beside Dylan. Maia peeked under the paper covering the box still in Dylan's arms.

"Wonderful," she said. "Tourist season will be here before we know it."

"Maia, you don't have to pretend for my sake. I know you're doing me a favor. Tourist season is months away."

"Nonsense." Her face pinked up. She nodded toward Dylan. "Who's your helper?"

Dylan had paused by a round table, a table with concentric shelves like a cake with layers, in the middle of the floor. He was staring at the shell creatures and the shell frames and the shell-encrusted crosses on those shelves. They were widely spaced. Kelli was glad to see the stock was low. That helped her ego a little bit.

"That's Dylan. Margie's nephew. Her sister's son."

He looked up at the sound of his name.

Maia said, "Of course. Nice to meet you, Dylan. Your aunt spoke of you. Did you get back before...we lost her?"

He shook his head. "No."

Kelli caught Dylan's eye. "Dylan, this is Maia. She runs the gallery. The Front Street Gallery is...was one of Margie's best customers."

Maia shook her head. "Your aunt was a very special, and talented, lady. We already miss her so much. Are you just visiting? Or will you be staying for a while?" She punctuated the question with a smile that showed her dimples.

The dimples worked on Dylan. He sort of grinned and looked aside, saying, "Not sure."

Maia nodded at the box he was holding. "You can set that on the table in the back."

Dylan left and Kelli followed Maia to the counter.

"How many do you have?" she asked.

Kelli told her and they discussed price. As

Maia was writing up the invoice, the sparkle of a diamond caught Kelli's attention.

"What's this?" She grabbed Maia's hand and turned it so the light danced across the faceted planes of the gem. "Oh, Maia." She glanced up at her friend's face.

Maia blushed fully this time.

"Who's the lucky guy? Do I know him?"

She shook her head. "He's not from around here."

"Is the date set?"

"Not yet. This feels pretty new still." Maia cast a surreptitious look at Dylan who had returned without the box and was standing at the large window with his back to them. "What about you two? He's nice looking in a hungry kind of way. Needs feeding, I think."

It sounded almost like a question. The feeding part. As for the first part, Kelli answered, "We've barely met. He came to visit his aunt, not realizing...you know."

"Oh, I see. That's too bad. You two look good together."

People in love wanted everyone else to be in love, too.

"I repeat, we hardly know each other."

The view beyond Dylan, in the direction in which he was staring, was of the shops that fronted on the sound and the marina to the left where they'd parked. This was a quiet time of year. After Christmas, the shops would scale back the hours. Again, she reminded herself of the favor Maia was doing for her. Kelli turned back to thank her again, but she was gone. She looked back at Dylan.

What had Maia seen in him? Broad shoulders, a little sharp. His hair was dark and untrimmed. His cheeks were rough with an ever-thickening growth of beard. A lot like the view she'd had of him yesterday on the back porch. He had nice cheekbones and a strong jaw....

Maia coughed softly. Kelli turned and she smiled, her eyes laughing.

"No," Kelli said.

"Of course not."

"I mean it."

"I don't doubt it." Maia handed her an envelope. "Here's the check and invoice. And listen, I don't mean to tease—or maybe I do, but only a little bit—seriously, you're suddenly alone. You're right to be cautious."

"I'm not a kid. You and I are the same age, Maia."

"Not quite the same. I'm a little ahead of you, I think. But it's not really about age, is it?"

"Whatever that means." The words sounded rude and Maia looked surprised, but

Kelli let them stand as said. "Thanks again, Maia."

She waved. Dylan followed her out of the door.

Whatever that means. Kelli knew what she meant. She meant experience. She meant women who hid themselves away from the world might not be smart about falling in love when the first likely-looking male came along. Especially if he was reasonably nice to her.

"What are you mad about?"

She spun around. Dylan was still up on the porch, looking down at her.

"I'm not mad."

He shrugged. "Have it your way. She seemed nice." He stepped lightly down the steps. "They had plenty of those shell things already. Why'd she buy more?"

"What? The table was almost empty."

"In the back room. There was a box full of them in the corner."

"You saw it?"

He shrugged. "I wasn't messing with their stuff. The box was under a stack of paper towel rolls. I bumped into them and they went everywhere. The paper towel rolls, I mean."

Kelli opened her mouth, then closed it again. She ran across the street and out of view of the gallery, she sat abruptly on a bench and hugged her knees, burying her face against the sleeves of her coat. She wouldn't cry. She wouldn't.

He touched her shoulder. "You okay?"

She dabbed at her eyes. She hadn't actually cried. Her lashes were just a little misty.

"I'm fine. Fine." It had felt less wrong to sell Margie's creatures when she thought the gallery could actually use them. She stood, stamped her feet, pulled her scarf closer and went to stand at the water's edge. "You see that?" She pointed across the sound.

"Out there? Water?"

"That water is Bogue Sound. Every spring, Margie and I take a boat ride across to Shackleford Banks to hunt shells and driftwood and smooth glass."

"Not this spring."

"No, not this spring." She started to say who knew where any of them would be by spring. But she pressed her lips together. She would be here. In Margie's house. Now Kelli's house. Hers. "You're wrong, Dylan. I'll be back at Shackleford Banks come spring and Margie will be with me." She put her hand to her heart. "Right here."

~*~

It was a quiet ride back to the house. Kelli parked in the back and neither of them spoke as they got out and went into the house. Finally, the heaviness of the silence was too much.

She remembered. "Oh, hey, guess what? Good news."

"Yeah? I like good news."

"The restaurant needs a part time assistant cook and dishwasher for a few days. Nothing fancy or anything, but they'll give you a try if you're interested. You can ride in and back with me each day. That's if they like your work. It can't hurt, right? Why not give it a chance?"

She smiled and the smile persisted even as his own faded. She couldn't grasp what the problem was.

"I told you no."

"But–"

"When you mentioned it before, I told you no."

She couldn't believe his attitude. "So you don't want a job?"

"I explained it already."

"You didn't have an address. On the street you can't wash up or dress up or whatever. Nobody wants to hire a homeless person. Well, you have an address now and the rest is meaningless."

He turned away, his arms tensing, his face a big scowl.

"Or maybe you just don't want a job. Not that kind of job. Kitchen work isn't good enough?"

"I have my own plans and I won't be here that long anyway. Don't waste your time."

"Really? Because I'm beginning to think your friend and his car are a total fiction. No one is coming for you. No one wants—"

The doorbell rang.

She froze. It had been how long? Ages? Since the front doorbell had last rung. Kelli didn't know it still worked. She rounded the corner from the kitchen to the front room and saw the outline of men. Two.

"Dylan?"

"What—"

"Are they here for you or me?" Had the authorities discovered she was living here with Margie gone? Who would care? The IRS maybe? Or was it about the Sullivan's house? Maybe they'd found evidence linking Dylan and followed him here.

"Answer the door."

"But—"

"Doesn't matter, Kelli. Just open the door."

"No. Be quiet." She clutched his sleeve. "They haven't seen us. They don't know we're here. They'll go away."

They stood. She gripped Dylan's forearm and willed the men to leave. She was terrified. She hadn't expected to be so frightened, and that frightened her all the more.

The men tucked something between the storm door and front door.

Kelli worked to breathe again. Her lungs had seized up. She gasped, trying to grab her breath back.

Dylan put his arm around her as he helped her over to the sofa.

"What was that about? Why would a couple of guys at the door upset you?"

"They might know...might know..." Breathe. "Margie's gone. I don't...I don't...this isn't my house." She waved her hands. "And the house up the street was broken into. Those men could've been cops asking questions."

"What are you talking about? A house was broken into? So what? Let them ask." He paused. "Did you...? Oh, you think it might have been me? Is that it?" He shook his head as Kelli tried to say no.

He said, "Don't worry about it."

She tried to drag the air back into her lungs. She'd said too much. Too, too much.

"You said Margie gave you the house." He

rubbed his hand over his face. "That wasn't true? I guess I can't blame you for lying."

"It wasn't a lie. It's about legalities. We can't find her will. Until I do, I can't prove it."

"Yeah?"

"I didn't lie."

"Lie? I don't know, but if not, it seems like you sure have a screwed-up idea of truth."

She covered her face with her hands, embarrassed. Not about the lack of perfect truthfulness but at her weakness, her fear. She'd made a fool of herself.

"Okay, get over it. You thought those guys were who? Cops? Here to haul you off? For what?"

"I don't know. Taxes? How long can I stay here without something going wrong? I need the will or I'm sunk."

"If no will is found, there's still an heir." He said it softly, thinking about it. "There's me. I'm her closest blood relative. As far as I know, I'm the only one."

And he was. That's why she'd wanted him to believe the house and she were a done deal. There was also the timing of Dylan's arrival with the break-in. Coincidental? Maybe. But even if he was innocent, it was just one more thing to worry about.

"Hey, it's okay. Really. Stop shaking."

He leaned against the back of the sofa and pushed the curtain slightly aside. "Gone. No one's out there. Relax."

Kelli nodded. If she truly believed he'd broken in and stolen from a nearby house—in fact, from a neighbor—would she try to protect him? Perhaps for Margie's sake? Or to shield herself from exposure?

He dropped back onto the sofa. His knee touched her thigh. She shivered.

"Why are you looking at me like that?"

"I don't know. My head is still spinning...What are you doing?"

"We can solve one question fast." He opened the front door. Papers fell onto the floor. He knelt to pick them up. "Flyers. Local church."

Kelli slumped back, the air whooshing out of her again. She heard Margie's voice saying she'd gotten ahead of herself with worry.

"Let's do something about it."

"About what?"

"The will. Whichever way it goes, it will be easier with the will. Are you sure she had one? Have you checked with her lawyer? She must've had a lawyer if she had a will."

"Not necessarily. Ron said they aren't required in North Carolina. A handwritten will with a couple of witnesses is enough. She had a lawyer friend and he might've helped her. Ron said he died last year. He's trying to locate the daughter to see if she has his old papers or knows anything. I think it's a long shot. If Margie made a will, whether a first or second will, then I think it's here in the house."

He frowned. "So if there's only one will, an early one, then I might be the heir? Margie told me when I was a kid…. But she had the right to change her mind. I don't hold it against her. If we find a more recent will, then it would be in your favor, right?"

She nodded.

"Well, then let's get looking."

"So you'd help look for it even if it hurts your claim?"

He shrugged. "Why not?"

She stared at his face. Was he trying to hide bad intentions? If he found it first would he hide it from her? Would he destroy it? She read no deception in his eyes nor in the set of his jaw and lips. She might have stared too long because something changed in his eyes as he looked back at her.

She jumped up from the sofa and tried not to run to the kitchen. She leaned against the counter. The years, all of the years she'd stayed with Margie—had hidden at Margie's house—seemed to have her by the throat. She was suffocating.

Almost thirty. In no time, she'd be in her forties. In a blink of the eye she'd be Margie. But without Margie's kindness and goodness. She'd just be alone and eccentric. Suddenly, the fight to keep Margie's house took on a different light, perhaps dimmed a bit. But home was still home, and she didn't have any other. Didn't want any other.

Dylan came into the kitchen. He paused, but without a word, he moved on. He went to his room as if there'd been no upheaval, and no connection snapping between them.

Maybe there hadn't been. Maybe she'd put off love and a relationship for so long that she imagined a connection where none existed.

~*~

The wind hit the house during the night with repeated thuds. It was a cruel wind that dug its fingers into every loose nook in the house. Dylan had the sleeping bag as an extra blanket in his small room. Kelli layered blankets over her blankets and snuggled in. Tomorrow would be a cold day. Sure as anything, the talk would start, each customer suggesting that just maybe, maybe they'd have a white Christmas. Christmas snow. It was rare here, but not impossible. She couldn't be sentimental about snow. It was an inconvenience, just like decorations and other holiday stuff.

Dylan mentioned Margie's tree at breakfast.

Kelli shut him down immediately. "No, it's a wreck. We're fine without a tree. Besides, isn't your friend arriving any day now? You won't be here."

"Good morning."

"I'm right, aren't I? When do you expect him?"

He shrugged. "You've decided I didn't make him up? I didn't have a phone number to give him. He's got Margie's address. He'll show up when he gets here. It's not like it'll take me long to pack." In a softer voice, he added, "Any time you want me to leave, just say so. I don't want to, but I will. Just say the word."

She eyed his jeans. One of two pair. One was worn, one was in the wash. "We should go to the church."

"We could, but I haven't noticed you beating down the church doors since I've been here."

"You've only been here two weeks."

"True. Seems longer, doesn't it?"

"For your information, they have a thrift bag at the church. With a little luck they'll have something that will fit you. Maybe we'll go over after work. After *my* work. I told them you weren't interested in the job." Kelli jumped up and grabbed her coat and scarf and bag and went to the back door. She slammed it behind her. Before she made it to the car, the door opened again and Dylan shouted, "I travel light. I have everything I need in my backpack. Anything else isn't worth the effort to carry or keep track of."

Dylan closed the back door before she could look away. She pulled her car door closed. She wanted to slam it, but it was an old car and all she had.

Needs in Dylan's life seemed few, too, and much more temporary.

Driving in, Kelli wondered what she'd been so angry about. Why would he ask about the tree? Not for himself. It was surely because he thought she'd like to have a Christmas tree which was sweet. She felt her anger heating up again. Easy enough for him to act all nice, but the truth of his sincerity was that he could hardly wait for his ride to arrive.

She wanted her life and home back, right? So she should be just as eager. But she wasn't.

~*~

When she came home from work, Dylan met her at the back door with a smirk on his face. Morning seemed long ago, her temper was spent, and she wasn't in the mood. She paused on the threshold. She didn't want to argue again. "What's up?"

He stood back. "Come on in."

She did, but looked around suspiciously.

"Lighten up, Kelli," he said, as he took her bag and scarf.

He'd cleared the table by the bookcase and set the piece of driftwood on top. A red hand towel was wrapped around the base. Two shells hung by string from the branches. Dylan picked up a dried starfish and offered it to her. She accepted it and turned it over. He'd fashioned a hanger by wrapping a thin piece of wire around one of the appendages and creating a loop on the back.

He nodded. "Well, go ahead."

He was grinning. It was contagious. She worked the wire loop over the topmost upright branch.

"Well?" he asked, pointing at the tree. "The silver stuff was falling off of Margie's tree. Made a mess. This needs more decoration, but it fits the beach, don't you think?"

It was gray and rangy, and the decorations were few and sad. Impulsively, Kelli reached out and took his hand in both of hers. "I think Margie would love it." And I do, too, she thought, but she stopped short of saying it aloud.

~*~

Kelli had the day off and Dylan wasn't here. Perhaps he was walking the beach and looking for work to fall from heaven. He was full of contradictions. Unemployed, but not lazy. He disappeared for hours at a time, but when he was here, he seemed glad of it and cooked and put up Christmas trees and such.

Mixed messages, she thought. Not from him, but in how she read them. He was taking life as it came. When his ride came, he'd blow out of town just as quietly as he'd arrived. She wasn't as laid back. She needed to remember he was a traveler at heart and this stay was temporary—just one more stop on his journey.

She walked down the crossover to scan the beach and Ron yelled her name. He was on his porch waving. Ah, so Dylan was there. She trotted down the steps and across the sand. As she reached Ron's stairs, he asked, "Have you seen Dylan?"

"No." Suddenly unsure, Kelli said, "I thought maybe he was working for you today."

"Nope. Haven't seen him in a few days. I do have something I could use some help with, so let him know? Okay?"

"Sure." Kelli walked a few steps closer so she could drop her voice lower. "I wanted to ask you about something."

"What can I help you with? Still no word from Sam Barrett's daughter."

"It's not that." She nodded up the strand. "I was thinking about the Sullivan's house, the break-in." She shrugged. "Just wondering if I needed to worry about anything?"

"Turned out it was the Sullivan's son taking an unexpected vacation from college. Heard he might've brought a friend or two with him. So, no break-in after all."

No break-in. She'd been pretty quick to suspect Dylan, although considering the coincidences and circumstances, she didn't blame herself for that. She was just sorry she'd let it slip in front of him.

And yet, where was he? She looked up the beach and down again. It was cold. Not unbearable, but still cold. Was he really walking? Who else was he doing jobs for? A twitch of suspicion made her look around at the houses up and down the beach.

She couldn't question him, not after that embarrassing breakdown in her living room.

Dylan wasn't a thief. She knew it. Whatever he was up to was his business.

Kelli had her own business to tend to. Margie's room.

She wasn't just trying to find the will. About that she didn't trust, or distrust him. It would just be better if she found it first. And she had to finish sorting through Margie's personal items and she preferred to do both jobs alone.

~*~

The flowered, ruffled pillow shams were faded and mended, as was the matching quilt. The books were still stacked on her dresser along with those last medicine bottles and mixed with shells, and a layer of dust coated it all.

Grief was understandable, but didn't necessarily represent respect. With this layer of dust, it looked a lot like neglect.

Kelli had boxes from the restaurant and a few bags. Most of Margie's clothing would go to the church, back to the thrift bag that Margie had such faith in. Anything too far gone for wear could be used as rags.

She sat on Margie's bed, then slowly sank

back into her pillows. She closed her eyes. Never would there ever be any way in which she could repay what Margie had done for her, and she'd done it with a smile and a loving heart.

At the time Kelli had ended up on Margie's porch, she was a teenager with nowhere to go. Like Dylan, She'd left a bad family situation and taken off on her own. Kelli and her mom didn't get along. Kelli had figured anywhere was better than where she was and she believed with all her heart that she was in love with a guy named Aaron. That last night, she'd yelled at her mother, "I'm out of here." Mom had answered, "Good." So she went. Mom didn't care; she had her own boyfriend. Maybe her mother thought Kelli would come back when she cooled off or got cold or scared or hungry. Mom was wrong. Wrong too many times.

It was a familiar story. Kelli believed hers ended better than most because she hadn't hung around long before she moved on. She didn't think so at the time, but she'd been lucky her boyfriend, Aaron, who turned out to be the boyfriend of many and who cared about none, had revealed himself so quickly. The night he decided to rob a convenience store and took her along for cover, was the end. The clerk was shot. In panic, she'd taken off and hadn't stopped. She'd kept moving and didn't fall into the darker lives of the underpasses and in the alleys. It wasn't because she was brave or smart. It was because she was scared.

Always on the move, afraid someone would recognize her face. Afraid Aaron would come looking for her. Or maybe the police. Her face would have been on the store video. She stayed off the main travel ways, staying below the radar and off the grid as much as possible. A scared mouse moving without much conscious thought way beyond the time and space when anyone anywhere would've been interested in where she was. Running was instinctive.

One day, she'd caught a lucky ride with an elderly woman. She was so harmless Kelli was lulled into dozing and when the car stopped, she opened her eyes to see the tall pole lights of a gas station. She sat up, with no idea where she was. The woman was inside the small convenience store and Kelli remembered why she was running. She got out of the car and left without a thank you. She took off down the road in the dark and found herself near a bridge over the sound. A long bridge with a graceful arc, and the water was alternately dark and glittering below. She thought it was a river. She found out later it was Bogue Sound. But she'd seen the ocean far beyond, a distant shimmering horizon, and she crossed the bridge.

To this day, to Kelli, the ocean represented a change in her circumstances. A change for the better. Maybe that's what it represented to Dylan—the time before his mother died, when he'd visited the aunt who doted on him—the best his world would ever be.

~*~

First, she emptied the closet of every last scrap of any kind. She piled the boxes and shoes on the floor and tossed the clothing and other assorted stuff onto the bed. Most of the shoes were old and very well worn. They'd be tossed.

Next, Kelli went through the drawers, more thoroughly than before and crying as she did. The memory of Margie wearing this item or that...the lingering scent...Kelli was nearly blind with tears. As a last consideration, just so she could say she checked everywhere, she moved the dresser. It was a heavy dresser and solid clear to where the bottom met the floor. It moved more easily than Kelli expected and behind it, not just dust bunnies were hiding. An envelope, long and white, and stuffed, was standing on end as if it had fallen from the top of the dresser and into the abyss between furniture and wall.

Maybe cleanliness did have its virtues.

Eagerly Kelli grabbed it, then held it, suddenly afraid. Dylan's name was written on the front.

What if Margie hadn't left the house to her, after all? Suppose she'd never gotten around to actually writing the second will? No, Ron had seen it. But the proof could be gone. Margie could've changed her mind and destroyed it.

Dylan wouldn't kick her out...but she wouldn't stay under those circumstances. It was different accepting charity from Margie when she was a teenager. She was an adult. So was he. If they were a couple...but they weren't. Heat rushed into her cheeks.

They barely knew each other. Still strangers, really.

She played with the sealed flap, teasing it.

His name was written on the envelope, clear and unmistakable, in Margie's handwriting. The envelope's return address was pre-stamped. An attorney. Sam Barrett.

She pressed the envelope to her chest, to her heart. If only she knew what the papers said. But they weren't hers. That wasn't her name on the envelope.

Who would know if she looked? No one would know she'd found it unless she told.

If, somehow, Margie did know, she might be disappointed, but she'd understand.

Kelli's face burned. She dropped the envelope and pressed her hands to her hot cheeks as the envelope hit the floor lightly, carelessly, as if might happen to slide under the bed...or maybe whoosh back behind Margie's dresser.

Would she lie?

What if...what if she'd never found it? The result would be the same.

Kelli fell to her knees and grabbed the envelope. How old? Hard to tell. And if she broke the seal, opened it and read it? If it was in her favor, how could she show it to Dylan? How could she explain why she'd opened something addressed to him?

He'd be gone in a few days. He need never know about it. Once he was on his way out of town, out of state, there'd be plenty of time for her to read it and decide what to do.

There was one problem with that plan. She'd still be herself, and she'd have to live with her choices. Could she?

She'd been here more than ten years. Her

haven. Her home. Now, Dylan was here and tired of traveling the roads alone, whether he wanted to admit it or not. That's why he'd come here. This was the closest thing to a home he'd ever had.

Kelli arranged the boxes neatly and labeled them and the bags. Most were destined for church. She kept one box of Margie's personal items. It was a big box, but a definite scaling down.

She took the wooden box, the one Margie had decorated and then wrapped around and around with a roll of red ribbon, and Dylan's envelope, and carried them to her room. The box went on the dresser. The envelope went into a drawer.

"Kelli?"

"Here."

He was standing in the hallway outside of Margie's room. "Wow. You've been busy."

He saw her face. "It was tough, huh? Your eyes..." He paused. "And I'm guessing by the look on your face that you didn't find any wills?"

Her mouth opened, then closed. She nodded, then said, "Yes. It was tough. But no, I didn't find what we were looking for."

~*~

Kelli held the guilt inside during supper and her tension probably dampened Dylan's mood, too, because he was quieter than usual. As they finished cleaning the supper dishes she said, "I'm really tired this evening. I'm heading to bed early." She didn't have to pretend. The sound of her voice would've convinced her, too, if she didn't already know the cause.

"Are you sick?"

She shook her head. "No." But she was. She was heartsick and in shock over what she'd done, and the fear she might do worse. The lies she'd told and her absolute willingness to tell more in order to keep the house, unnerved her. And she was willing to do it to someone else's detriment.

"I should've been here to help you. It was too much to take it on by yourself."

Guilt slapped her. "I managed." After a pause and a breath, she added, "Sorry."

"You never told me how you came to be here with Margie."

"No, I didn't."

He waited.

"It was a long time ago."

"You were still a kid, right? A teenager. It's different when you've been traveling for so many years."

"Traveling."

"Yes. So you ran away from home?"

"I left home. Didn't have to run. No one tried to stop me. No one came looking for me." Suddenly the defensiveness seemed pointless. "It's a common story. Mom got a new boyfriend. He and I didn't get along. Mom kept the boyfriend."

"I don't think she believed I'd stay gone. I went to a friend's house, but it didn't work out and so I left. It went downhill from there." She shook her head, refusing to mention Aaron. "I made it here by chance. Margie would say God brought me to her porch. But either way, the road I travelled to get here was hard and scary and hungry, with lots of predators along the way." In truth, it had been awful, but the memories, the feelings had dimmed over the decade of safe, soft living. She was grateful and wanted the memories to keep fading. But she was also an adult now and she had a work history, an identity. She could make it on her own. She could.

"You're smiling," he said.

"You're right," she said. "I put all the crap behind me a long time ago. I stopped being that lost kid a long time ago."

~*~

She lay in the dark, not wanting to think about it, but it wouldn't go away. She had to figure it out now or she'd get no rest. She needed rest. Tomorrow was shaping up to be a life altering, game changer of a day.

The thin line of light beneath her door winked out. Dylan had called it a night, too.

He had come home to his Aunt Margie to reclaim the few good memories of his childhood from someone who loved him, someone who was guaranteed not to turn him away. He came because he was tired of the traveling life.

Kelli rolled over and wrapped her arms around her second pillow. She stared at the closed bedroom door. She'd stopped moving the dresser in front of it. Not for the first time, she wondered what she'd do if Dylan knocked.

Which was another reason why it was time to move on. They couldn't both stay. She, Kelli, didn't want the day to come when she found out Dylan was no different from any other guy. That in an unguarded moment, the light would hit him just right and he'd look like the ones she'd worked so hard to forget.

The worst was that ugly splotch on her past—not from Aaron or anyone else—only from her. How she'd left the clerk bleeding on the floor. Hadn't stopped to help him, hadn't called the police. That was all on her and she couldn't fix it so she hid it. Like chains holding her. She couldn't pay it backward.

Suddenly, she knew without a doubt— Dylan didn't have a friend coming. It was a cover for his pride. Christmas was almost here. Three days away. He'd be here on Christmas day because it was fate and it was a good thing because she had a gift for him. The gift she'd received twelve years ago. It was time to return it. Sort of a re-gift. A closed circle. Fate. A gift to him from Margie.

~*~

Kelli spent the next day thinking about what she'd take with her. Not much. As Dylan had said, less was more when traveling. At least she had the car because her days of traveling by foot were long done. Gas money might get tight, but one day at a time, she told herself.

"What's wrong with you, Kelli?"

Mr. Beale. She'd nearly knocked him over.

"Nothing. Sorry."

"You sick?"

She shook her head. "No, I'm good." The door opened and customers walked in. She turned to greet them, glad of the rescue from Mr. Beale's sharp eyes.

Destinations flitted through her mind. North or south on I-95 was the obvious, so maybe west? Nowhere was out of the question, except perhaps her hometown. No temptation to return there.

Suddenly, it flashed into her head that she had to give notice. She stopped. With one couple just seated and another walking in through the front door, she'd frozen. Leaving meant leaving this job, too. It took her breath away. The finality of it.

Someone gripped her arm.

"Kelli?" Mr. Beale prompted.

She pressed her hand to her forehead. Lightheaded. That was all.

"Sit down." He moved her along until she was clear of the main aisle. "Excuse us, please."

At a table far in the back, no one around, Mr. Beale brought her a glass of water. "Drink this."

Kelli wrapped her hands around the glass and forced herself to focus, to breathe.

"Go home, Kelli. Sick or not, something's wrong. This isn't the place for it. Can you drive? Is there someone I can call?"

"No, I'm okay."

"You aren't. Go home. If you aren't feeling better tomorrow, take the day off. We'll be short-handed, but we'll manage."

She hoped they would because she didn't know how to tell him she wasn't coming back.

~*~

Kelli had left work early and arrived home early. Dylan wasn't there.

Tomorrow was Christmas Eve and he was planning a special dinner. She'd leave Christmas Day, early when the traffic would be light. Instead of rising pre-dawn for her morning beach walk, it would be a much shorter walk to her car.

Kelli stopped by the bookcase and pressed her hands against the sides of the urn.

"Goodbye. Thank you, Margie."

In Margie's room, she took a last look. In the box marked, keep, there were a few items, knick-knacks and photos, that Dylan might like. For herself, Kelli, she was done. Almost.

Chapter Four

Christmas Eve. She went to work. It was habit.
It was an obligation. Plus, she didn't want to
hang around the house.

Kelli smiled when she greeted Mr. Beale
who was clearly relieved to see her. As lunch
crept along, it became clear the restaurant
was like a dead zone, practically echoing in its
emptiness. Even most of the regulars didn't
drop in. She stood at the plate glass window.
The others were examining the overcast sky
watching for the first flakes to fall.

It was cold enough, but no forecasts were
calling for snow. There weren't many white
Christmases here on the island.

Kelli breathed and the glass fogged up.
She wrote a D in it, then remembered she
wasn't twelve and used her sweater to scrub it
away. Why get all goofy now? After a night's
sleep, and with decisions made, she felt
calmer. Her suitcase was packed, mostly. As
soon as this shift was over, she'd head back
to the house, endure the special supper Dylan
was going to prepare, get up in the wee hours
of the night and drive away. And somewhere
in there, she had to tell Dylan the truth and

give him Margie's envelope.

As the afternoon wore on, Nadia said, "We're closing early."

"We never close early. The weather is fine."

"Not for the weather. Seriously, Kelli, no one will notice. This place is a tomb today."

Mr. Beale said, "I'm flipping the sign. Do the pickup and the setup and then go. Merry Christmas."

Quietly, Kelli slipped into his office, placed a note on his desk, and left.

~*~

Kelli parked and went inside. The house was nearly dark. She'd expected to find him home. Not one light was on.

"Dylan?"

She went to his room. The bed was made. His backpack was in the corner. She breathed a long sigh of relief, then realized her stupidity. If he left...well, then that would've made her own decision unnecessary.

It was sobering to consider it. She'd learned some unhappy truths about herself and going back to the way her life had been before Dylan arrived, was no longer possible.

Better if he'd never come. But that felt unthinkable.

She lost either way. Or maybe she'd won because, in the end, one had to face one's past in order to move forward.

Kelli went to her room and switched on the light. She put Maggie's ancient suitcase on the bed, undid the latches and did a quick check. Anxiety perhaps, but suddenly she was thinking of more things she'd need. She closed her eyes, breathed slowly and cleared her mind. When it came right down to it, people didn't need all that much.

She heard the creak of the front door and a step in the hallway.

"Kelli?"

She grabbed the bedspread and yanked it back over the suitcase, then threw some clothing on top to disguise the shape.

"In here," she responded, and went directly to the doorway. She saw his face. "What happened?"

Dylan rubbed his clean cheeks and chin. "If you miss it, I can grow it back."

"No," she said. "It suits you." She gave him another look. "In fact, you look happy."

He grinned. "Is that so unusual?" He laughed. "Okay. It is. I've got good news."

"So share."

"Not yet." He put out his hands in a stopping motion. "I have to start cooking."

"How much did you spend for the food? I don't mind paying."

Dylan shook his head. "Not a chance. This dinner is my Christmas gift to you."

His excitement warmed her. She wanted to join in the upbeat mood, but it felt dishonest. Or was it selfish not to? He had a happy surprise. The least she could do was to let him enjoy the mood for a little while.

"You haven't said yet what's on the menu." A grocery bag was on the counter. She reached toward it. "How'd you get to the store anyway?"

"Ron drove me. And hands off. No spoiling the surprise."

Ron and Dylan seem to have taken to each other. One more reason to let him have the house.

"Okay, okay." She pointed toward Margie's room. "I was going to finish the cleanup and packing in Margie's room. I'll get out of your way."

He laughed. It was good to hear his laughter and to see the laugh lines at the corners of his eyes come alive. She felt her own smile grow. Too bad it couldn't last.

She paused just inside Margie's room and leaned against the wall.

Time to get on with it.

She opened a drawer and another. Opened and closed the closet door. Just enough noise to reassure Dylan and allow him to lose himself in his cooking, then she returned to her own room and eased the door shut.

What about the things she wasn't taking? She hadn't really considered that. Not that she had a bunch of stuff, but more than she could take on the road. She began shoving keepsakes and various items into the sides of the suitcase and in between the clothing. Her tension grew into a brittleness of spirit. She retrieved Dylan's envelope from the drawer, almost angry, and she tossed it on the bed next to the suitcase. She was leaving, in part, because she'd been tempted not to give it to him. Had even lied about it. So, before she left, she'd put it where he'd find it. Maybe under the driftwood tree? That was appropriate for a Christmas gift.

She stacked old papers on the bed, notes and old receipts, to go in the trash. She put some extra clothing and spare shoes into a plastic bag. She waited until she was near the back door to call out, "Dylan? I'll be right back. I left something in the car." She was out the door before he responded. She put the bags in the trunk and then eased the lid down as quietly as she could. In about twelve hours, more or less, she'd be on the road to her future.

She grabbed the pile of papers from the bed—who knew she could accumulate so much pointless paper—then dragged the bedspread back over the suitcase. She went into the kitchen and dropped the papers into the trashcan.

Dylan's long lashes fringed his black eyes, concentrating his stare as he focused on the cooking. She tried to look away, but her gaze fell on his hands. Strong hands. He sliced the potatoes and added them to the pot and ran the water over them.

She watched him. He checked in a bag. Looked in the fridge. Clearly, he was searching for something.

"Can I help?"

Suddenly his hands moved. He hit the counter lightly with his fist.

"I forgot something," he said. His voice carried the sound of doom. Her heart clinched. Now what?

"I left a bag at Ron's house. In his car, I'll bet."

"All that for a forgotten bag? Want me to go fetch it from Ron?"

"No," he said, giving her a quick smile. "I'll get it. Keep an eye on the potatoes? When the water comes to a boil cut the heat back halfway."

"I can do that."

What a strange man. Such a hard-looking man, and yet so wrapped up in cooking a special meal, worrying over the ingredients and stuff.

Kelli picked up the spoon and gave the potatoes a light stir to keep them from settling on the bottom.

The door. Someone knocked. The back door, in fact. He'd gone out one way and come back the other. The door was locked. Dylan must not have his key. She ran to open it, but it wasn't Dylan.

"Hello, there."

A man. A stranger.

Her face was flushed from the steam of the boiling potatoes, not for this stranger and his ready smile. She stepped back, wanting to slam the door, knowing she couldn't.

He put his hand on the door. "I startled you. Sorry."

She stared at his hand and he pulled it back.

"I'm looking for my friend. Dylan. Is he here?" He added. "He's expecting me."

The ride.

The surprise. The good news. The after-dinner news that Dylan was so excited to share. Here it was on her doorstep.

"Did I interrupt something? I probably did, being Christmas Eve and all. Did Dylan tell you I was on my way?"

She stammered, "No, yes, I mean."

The front door squeaked open and thudded closed.

"Got it, Kelli."

"Got it?" The man repeated. "Kelli?" He smiled and called out, "Dylan? That you?"

"John. You made it."

Dylan walked past her and she stepped back as his friend, John, crossed the threshold. They did some shoulder and back slapping.

"We were just pulling supper together. Come on in."

He flashed a smile again. "Just in time, I guess."

Dylan was saying, "How was the drive?" as they walked into the kitchen. Kelli stayed in the hallway. She heard Dylan set the bag he'd retrieved on the kitchen counter. Someone opened the fridge.

She had no wish to join them. Stunned, she grabbed her coat from the wall hook on her way to the front door.

The wind had slackened to a light onshore

breeze, but it had an icy touch that chilled her. First, her cheeks, then the rest of her face and her ears. She shoved her hands into her pockets. She welcomed the cold.

The sky was clear, so there'd be no snow for Christmas. Never'd been any real chance of it anyway. People were just crazy-headed dreamers about sentimental things like that. She sniffled. Her nose was growing numb.

So this had been Dylan's surprise. His ride had arrived.

"Kelli?"

"Oh, hey, Dylan." Casual. Oh so carefully casual.

He came out to the porch.

"What a surprise, huh?" he said.

"Yes. Quite a surprise." She wouldn't add that it was almost insulting that he'd seemed so eager about it earlier. So eager to leave Margie's house, those memories he'd pretended were precious, and leaving her, too. "Where is he?"

"He went on a beer run. Grocery store or convenience store. Told him I wasn't sure what was open. It's Christmas Eve, after all."

She shifted her freezing feet. "Well, who can blame him, right? When you gotta have beer, you gotta have it, I guess. He's your friend, not mine."

"What's wrong?"

"Nothing. I'm fine." There was no point in speaking her mind. She was leaving in a few hours. But no. His ride was here. He was leaving. She gulped. "I just need some air."

"I have to check on the roast. Come back in where it's warm."

"I will."

He went inside. She put her hands to her head. She was so confused. Was he leaving or not? They had to figure this out. She went inside and to the kitchen. "Dylan."

He turned abruptly and knocked a bag off the counter. It fell into the trashcan. "The mushrooms. Portabellas." He said the word as if he could taste it. He picked up the trashcan and began digging through it. He pulled out the bag and a piece of paper. "What's this? Is this yours, Kelli? Did you mean to throw it away?"

"Yes, I was going through some old stuff. It's trash."

He dropped it back into the can, but his hand came back up with something else. "What's this?" He turned it toward her. "It has my name on it. Why is it in the trash can?"

Kelli shook her head. "No, it wasn't in the trash can. I mean, it wasn't so I don't know how it got there. I was going to give it to you."

He looked at it again, at his name on it. The

envelope was stained from something it had touched in the trash. He released the trashcan.

"When?"

"Later." She gestured toward the trashcan. "I don't know how it got in there."

"No. I'm asking when you found it."

The silence was long. Kelli wanted to stop it from stretching between them because the longer the silence stretched, the more impossible it was for her to answer without the words sounding like a lie. Lies and lies and lies.

"Two days ago," she said.

"You told me you didn't find anything."

She had no acceptable answer.

He shook his head. He slapped his hand with the envelope, then held the paper up. "This was important. It was so important for me to see that you decided it was important to hide?" He closed his eyes and when he opened them, he added, "You threw it away, so I wouldn't find it."

Anger arced like electricity between hot wires in her brain. "Don't judge me. Who are you anyway? You're the guy who can't wait to leave. You pushed your way in, turned my life upside down, and what was your big, exciting news today? The news you could hardly wait to share? Your ride is here. Your ride! Hah, you ride in and you ride back out and in-between you screw up everything. I never asked you here. I never asked you to stay. So just go ahead and be happy about leaving, and leave me alone."

Dylan ripped the envelope open and pulled the papers free. He threw them in the air and they fluttered to the floor. "Here. For you. Be happy. It's all yours with my blessing."

He came close and said, "That surprise? It was about the job I got. A cook at a restaurant in town. It's a long walk both ways and I'm only there on trial, but that's where I've been going, proving to them I'm worth keeping on until the tourists come back." He banged his fist on the table. "Stupid. Just stupid."

The back door slammed and they both jumped. John was back. He walked into the kitchen like he owned the place. Dylan turned away, saying, "You wanted me gone and now my ride is here. That's right, isn't it, Kelli? Merry Christmas."

Kelli was too stunned to speak. She ran to the front door, back out to the porch. She stopped at the railing and clung to it. *Please go, Dylan. Please don't go. Please follow me out here.* She could go back inside, ignore his friend, ignore her pride, and ask Dylan to stay and work it out. Maybe one of them didn't have to leave…maybe.

In the silence, she heard men's voices, noises and then a door slamming. Had John left? Dylan? He'd said it before—it wouldn't take him long to pack.

It might not be a white Christmas, but in her heart, and on her frosty cheeks, the tears felt as bitter as an ice storm.

~*~

Dylan hadn't brought much and had accumulated almost nothing. His contributions to the house had been some minor fix-its, but mostly cooking, and they'd eaten that. There was also the Christmas driftwood on the table with the silly shells dangling from the dead branches, and a dead starfish on top. That pretty much summed up the recent weeks of her life. In fact, all of the weeks since Margie's death.

She stood at the door not wanting to enter the empty house, but the aroma of the baking roast drew her into the kitchen. Dylan had turned the oven off. He'd cut off the fire under the pots, too. Thanks, Dylan. Safety first.

The unused dishes, their two place settings, were still at the table. Unused.

Let it sit, she told herself. All of it. Let it rot. She wasn't hungry.

Kelli went to her bedroom. The clothing and bedspread hadn't done much to conceal the shape of the open suitcase beneath, but it had done well enough since Dylan hadn't entered her room. She was tired. So very tired. But she couldn't bear the sight of the suitcase, so she left it covered for now. There was no offer of rest in this room, this bed, tonight.

In the small back room, Dylan's bed was still made, but his backpack was gone. Of course.

She'd won, hadn't she?

That left Margie's room. She sat on the edge of the bed. Not long ago, she had curled up here and mourned Margie. Tonight, Kelli needed comfort, but there was none. The bed was stripped, and the boxes were stacked. Margie was gone.

She wanted a do-over of the last few days. At least of this evening. But do-overs didn't happen in real life.

Kelli began to cry, and it grew into ugly wrenching sobs. Grief, loss, anger, fear. It hurt to breathe. She forced air past the spasms in her chest as small lights danced across her vision. By the time the storm subsided, she was flat on the floor with no will to get back up.

And no reason to except the floor was hard and she was getting cold.

She grabbed a pillow from her bed and took Margie's box, the one she'd decorated for Kelli's Christmas gift. Dylan's letter, too. She gathered the pages from the floor and folded them as well as she could. The roast was cool now. She covered it in plastic wrap. She'd get a few meals out of it, and the gravy and potatoes, too. With only her to eat them, they'd last a while. No point in wasting the food.

With every other room being inhospitable, Kelli arranged her pillow, blanket and stuff on the sofa, realizing too late, after she was already settled in, that she was facing Dylan's tree. Maybe the direction hadn't been intentional, and maybe not a mistake either.

Dylan's tree. Driftwood. Prophetic in a way. And on the bookcase, the urn sat, like a reproach.

She curled up against the pillow with the box cradled on her lap. She pushed aside some of the red ribbons and traced the shells on the box with her finger, imagining Margie's own nimble fingers arranging the shells and wielding the glue gun like an old master's paint brush. Kelli rubbed the smooth petals of mother of pearl. Margie had worked on the box while Kelli was at work or asleep. Margie had chosen these shells, had arranged them with love. On the blanket near Kelli's arm was Dylan's letter. She'd done half of the right thing. She hadn't opened it, but she also hadn't given it to him. She would have, right? She hoped so, but she wasn't sure.

She knew without doubt she was exhausted. Her last thought as she fell asleep was of the place settings at the table. The Christmas Eve dinner uneaten. Dinner for two.

If he'd been expecting his friend, his ride, why hadn't there been three plates?

In the pre-dawn hours of Christmas Day, she dreamed. Margie was in the kitchen cooking. No, not Margie. Dylan was cooking, humming to the tune of the kitchen noises. Kelli kept sleeping because as long as the dream state held, she could be part of it. She could pretend it was real as long as she didn't wake up.

Fingers touched her forehead, cool against her flesh, against her cheek. Then his lips brushed hers, but gently, and she wanted the dream to go on, but then his face changed. It became that of his friend, John, then the dreaded face of the boyfriend from a lifetime ago. The kiss dissolved as she struggled to open her eyes and scream, ready to fight. One more time.

"Kelli. Hush. It's okay."

Dylan's hands were on her shoulders. Not restraining. He was drawing her closer, into his arms. "You were dreaming. A nightmare maybe." He sat back and looked into her eyes. "Are you okay?"

She touched his face. Her fingers, her hands were busy moving over his cheeks, through his hair. His flesh was cold. Icy.

"Are you real?"

He grabbed her hand. "I'm real. I'm back."

She shook her head. "No. Why are you back?" She held her breath.

"This is home. As far as I'm concerned it's your home and I'm hoping you'll let me stay."

"Dylan, did you kiss me?" she whispered.

He frowned and smiled at the same time. He spoke in a low voice. "No, I didn't, but I'm happy to anytime you're willing."

Kelli pressed her free hand against the back of his head, feeling his hair, the solid strength of his neck and shoulders, then pulled his face forward until her lips touched his.

When she released him, he noticed the box on her lap. "What's this?"

"It's a box I gave Margie for Christmas. An early Christmas present, so she could decorate it for me, for Christmas. I know it sounds silly."

Dylan took the box. He held it and said, "I know it's just shells glued to a wooden box, but Kelli, this is like a work of art. I'm not so sure about the wrapping job."

"Margie was very talented and what she did, she did with love." She paused. "Dylan, I hope you'll forgive me and understand I was afraid."

He gave her the box back. "I was afraid, too. Otherwise, I would've told you what I was up to. I didn't expect the job to work out. I didn't want to have to admit it if it didn't."

She looked around, hugging the box. "Where's John? Your friend?"

He laughed. "Not here. That's why it took me so long to get back. I wanted him out of here."

"But you were glad to see him. You left with him."

Dylan scratched his head, ruffling his thick black hair. Kelli reached up and without thinking, smoothed some of it back away from his face. His eyes, dark as ever, lit up. His face, his entire aspect, became quiet. Still. That was the only way she could describe it. Even his voice softened.

"I had just about convinced myself John was never going to show up here. I was glad. And when he did, yes, I left with him, but I knew I was coming back, angry or not. You and I had things that needed saying. But a guy like John...you can't just tell him to leave. He might, or he might not, and I didn't want to waste time hassling with him. When I figured he'd driven beyond where he'd want to turn back. I started an argument. Not hard with guys like him. He put me out on the side of the road. I watched the tail lights vanish over the rise and I started the walk back. Not many ride opportunities late on Christmas Eve and I was worried about whether you'd let me in. It was late, but then I remembered that this time I had a key. It was a long walk back and look, it's already Christmas Day."

He pushed the curtain aside. The sun wasn't up yet, but the early light was growing.

"You walked for hours?" She touched his face.

"I've been walking for years."

"I should've given you this sooner." She offered him the envelope. "Why don't we open it officially together?"

He smiled. He pulled the papers out of the envelope. That poor envelope had suffered and so had the papers. Dylan looked through them.

"Well, you were right. ...leave my home and property, etc...to my nephew..." His voice trailed off as he examined the document. "Dated the year my mother died."

"So now we know. The house is yours. Yours to do what–"

"Wait," Dylan said. "I don't care about the house. That's what I said, and I meant it."

Kelli started to speak. He touched her cheek and hair. "Let me finish?"

"When I came back I went to your room. I knew you'd be sleeping and I didn't want to scare you. But you weren't there, and I saw the suitcase. Were you going to leave?" He didn't wait for an answer. "I don't want the house without you. I'm serious. If you leave, I leave. What's a house if it's empty of the people you care about, the ones you love?"

Love. He'd said the word. But not for her. He'd meant that word for his aunt.

"We hardly know each other."

"Is that true, really? We've both waited a long time to find love. You trusted me with your life by letting me in the house that first morning. Don't think I don't know that. If you can put up with me, and if I can walk many, many miles on a cold winter night to find my way back to you, then I think I can be patient while we get to know each other better. I think maybe we can live a lifetime and never finish getting to know each other."

Kelli's heart, her breath…everything seemed to stop. The room began to tip and Dylan leaned forward to steady her.

"Ouch," he said. "That box again."

The wooden box with its sharp corners was still on her lap. When she moved, the box began to slide. Margie's shells, the red ribbons slipping and moving, she foresaw the box hitting the floor, the shells cracking…

Dylan grabbed it. He caught it by one of the ribbons which untied and unrolled like a tiny red carpet as the box continued at a slower pace toward the floor. As it hit, the lid opened and papers fell partway out.

"What's this?" he asked. He reached for them and Kelli grabbed his arm.

"Wait."

"Why?"

"Because I'm happy right now. I don't want to risk that changing."

"You're afraid."

"I'm not, but I know that when things are good, it won't last. You have to hold on to the good stuff as hard as you can."

He shook his head. "You aren't happy."

"I am."

"You aren't. If you were, you wouldn't be afraid a few pieces of paper could upset that, especially papers put there by your best friend for you to find at Christmas."

She put her feet on the floor and sat up straighter. She held the papers as if they were everything and forever, and she held them unopened as if they were nothing. She closed her eyes.

"You can read better with your eyes open." He touched her arm. "Kelli, it's the later will. The one Ron saw."

"Probably."

"Kelli?"

She stared at him. "Will we make it, Dylan? It won't be easy. Life isn't, and this house, Margie's house, needs so much work."

"I don't mind."

"I don't either, but there are realities we have to deal with."

"Better together than alone."

She smiled. "Okay, you win." She unfolded the papers. "Yes, here's the will. And what's this? A life insurance policy. She left a life insurance policy. A big one." Her hands dropped to her lap, her fingers holding the papers. "She had it all figured out, didn't she, Dylan?"

He put his arm around her and pressed his lips to her temple. When he sat back, he said, "No, I don't think she did, but I think she did have faith it would all work out. Margie never let worry or fear rule her life, did she? And we won't either."

Kelli rose, placing the box and papers on the coffee table.

"Where are you going?"

"For my beach walk." She pulled the blanket around her. "I may only go as far as the porch, but I want to see the sunrise this morning with you."

They went out into the cold and stood on the crossover, shivering.

"I thought love was supposed to be enough to keep you warm." She laughed.

Dylan wrapped his arm around her and pulled her close. "Sometimes you need a warm coat and shoes, too." He added, "And a gorgeous sunrise."

"The clouds make it more colorful, but they don't look like snow clouds. I guess it's no snow for Christmas again this year."

"Were you hoping for snow? A white Christmas here at the beach?"

Kelli shook her head. "Well, there's always hope, but if not this year, maybe next. I believe we have lots of Christmases ahead of us."

The End

ABOUT THE AUTHOR

Stories of heart and hope ~ from the Outer Banks to the Blue Ridge

USA Today Bestselling and award-winning author, Grace Greene, writes novels of contemporary romance with sweet inspiration, and women's fiction with romance, mystery and suspense.

A Virginia native, Grace has family ties to North Carolina. She writes books set in both locations. The Emerald Isle, NC Stories series of romance and sweet inspiration are set in North Carolina. The Virginia Country Roads novels, and the Cub Creek novels have more romance, mystery, and suspense.

Grace lives in central Virginia. Stay current with Grace's news at www.gracegreene.com.

You'll also find Grace here:
http://twitter.com/Grace_Greene
https://www.facebook.com/GraceGreeneBooks
http://www.goodreads.com/Grace_Greene

Other Books by Grace Greene

If you enjoyed BEACH WALK, you might enjoy these novels:

BEACH RENTAL (Emerald Isle #1)

RT Book Reviews – Sept. 2012 - 4.5 stars TOP PICK

No author can even come close to capturing the awe-inspiring essence of the North Carolina coast like Greene. Her debut novel seamlessly combines hope, love and faith, like the female equivalent of Nicholas Sparks. ...you'll hear the gulls overhead and the waves crashing onto shore.

Brief Description:

On the Crystal Coast of North Carolina, in the small town of Emerald Isle...

Juli Cooke, hard-working and getting nowhere fast, marries a dying man, Ben Bradshaw, for a financial settlement, not expecting he will set her on a journey of hope and love. The journey brings her to Luke Winters, a local art dealer, but Luke resents the woman who married his sick friend and warns her not to hurt Ben—and he's watching to make sure she doesn't.
Until Ben dies and the stakes change.
Framed by the timelessness of the Atlantic Ocean

and the brilliant blue of the beach sky, Juli struggles against her past, the opposition of Ben's and Luke's families, and even the living reminder of her marriage—to build a future with hope and perhaps to find the love of her life—if she can survive the danger from her past.

BEACH WINDS (Emerald Isle #2)

Brief Description:

Off-season at Emerald Isle ~ In-season for secrets of the heart

Frannie Denman has been waiting for her life to begin. After several false starts, and a couple of broken hearts, she ends up back with her mother until her elderly uncle gets sick and Frannie goes to

Emerald Isle to help manage his affairs.

Frannie isn't a 'beach person,' but decides her uncle's home, *Captain's Walk,* in winter is a great place to hide from her troubles. But Frannie doesn't realize that winter is short in Emerald Isle and the beauty of the ocean and seashore can help heal anyone's heart, especially when her uncle's handyman is the handsome Brian Donovan.

Brian has troubles of his own. He sees himself and Frannie as two damaged people who aren't likely to equal a happy 'whole' but he's intrigued by this woman of contradictions.

Frannie wants to move forward with her life. To do that she needs questions answered. With the right information there's a good chance she'll be able to affect not only a change in her life, but also a change of heart.

THE MEMORY OF BUTTERFLIES
(Lake Union Women's Fiction)
Brief Description:
A young mother lies to keep a devastating family secret from being revealed, but the lies, themselves, could end up destroying everything and everyone she loves. Hannah Cooper's daughter, Ellen, is leaving for college soon. As Ellen's high school graduation approaches, Hannah decides it's time to return to her roots in Cooper's Hollow along Virginia's beautiful and rustic Cub Creek. Hannah's new beginning comes with unanticipated risks that will

cost her far more than she ever imagined—perhaps more than she can survive.

THE HAPPINESS IN BETWEEN
(Lake Union Women's Fiction)
Brief Description:
Sandra Hurst has left her husband. Again. She's made the same mistake twice and her parents refuse to help this time—emotionally or financially. Desperate to earn money and determined to start over, she accepts an offer from her aunt to house-sit at the old family home, Cub Creek, in beautiful rural Virginia. But when Sandra arrives, she finds the house is shabby, her aunt's dog is missing, and the garden is woefully overgrown. And she suspects her almost-ex-husband is on her trail. Sandra needs one more change at regaining her self-respect, making peace with her family, and discovering what she's truly made of.

KINCAID'S HOPE (Virginia Country Roads)

<u>RT Book Reviews</u> – Aug. 2012 - 4 STARS

A quiet, backwater town is the setting for intrigue, deception and betrayal in this exceptional sophomore offering. Greene's ability to pull the reader into the story and emotionally invest them in the characters makes this book a great read.

<u>Jane Austen "Book Maven"</u> - May 2012 - 5 STARS

This is a unique modern-day romantic suspense novel, with eerie gothic tones—a well-played combination, expertly woven into the storyline.

<u>Brief Description</u>:

Beth Kincaid left her hot temper and unhappy childhood behind and created a life in the city free from untidy emotionalism, but even a tidy life has danger, especially when it falls apart.

In the midst of her personal disasters, Beth is called back to her hometown of Preston, a small town in southwestern Virginia, to settle her guardian's estate. There, she runs smack into the mess she'd left behind a decade earlier: her alcoholic father, the long-ago sweetheart, Michael, and the poor opinion of almost everyone in town.

As she sorts through her guardian's possessions, Beth discovers that the woman who saved her and raised her had secrets, and the truths revealed begin to chip away at her self-imposed control.

Michael is warmly attentive and Stephen, her ex-fiancé, follows her to Preston to win her back, but it is the man she doesn't know who could forever end Beth's chance to build a better, truer life.

A STRANGER IN WYNNEDOWER

(Virginia Country Roads)

– January 2013 - 5 STARS

I loved this book! It is Beauty and the Beast meets mystery novel! The story slowly drew me in and then there were so many questions that needed answering, mysteries that needed solving! ...Sit down and relax, because once you start reading this book, you won't be going anywhere for a while! Five stars for a captivating read!

Brief Description:

Love and suspense with a dash of Southern Gothic...

Rachel Sevier, a lonely thirty-two-year-old inventory specialist, travels to Wynnedower Mansion in Virginia to find her brother who has stopped returning her calls. Instead, she finds Jack Wynne, the mansion's bad-tempered owner. He isn't happy to meet her. When her brother took off without notice, he left Jack in a lurch.

Jack has his own plans. He's tired of being responsible for everyone and everything. He wants to shake those obligations, including the old mansion. The last thing he needs is another complication, but he allows Rachel to stay while she waits for her brother to return.

At Wynnedower, Rachel becomes curious about the house and its owner. If rumors are true, the means to save Wynnedower Mansion from demolition are hidden within its walls, but the other inhabitants of Wynnedower have agendas, too. Not only may Wynnedower's treasure be stolen, but also the life of its arrogant master.

CUB CREEK
(Virginia Country Roads)

Brief Description:

In the heart of Virginia, where the forests hide secrets and the creeks run strong and deep ~

Libbie Havens doesn't need anyone. When she chances upon the secluded house on Cub Creek she buys it. She'll prove to her cousin Liz, and other doubters, that she can rise above her past and live happily and successfully on her own terms.

Libbie has emotional problems born of a troubled childhood. Raised by a grandmother she could never please, Libbie is more comfortable *not* being comfortable with people. She knows she's different from most. She has special gifts, or curses, but are they real? Or are they products of her history and dysfunction?

At Cub Creek Libbie makes friends and attracts the romantic interest of two local men, Dan Wheeler and Jim Mitchell. Relationships with her cousin and other family members improve dramatically and Libbie experiences true happiness—until tragedy occurs.

Having lost the good things gained at Cub Creek, Libbie must find a way to overcome her troubles, to finally rise above them and seize control of her life and future, or risk losing everything, including herself.

~*~

BEACH WALK is part of the Emerald Isle, NC Stories Series and is also written as a standalone, or single title. If you are interested in reading the entire series, here is the recommended reading order:

BEACH RENTAL is the first book in the series.

The short story, BEACH TOWEL, references a scene in BEACH RENTAL.

BEACH WINDS is the second novel in the Emerald Isle, NC Stories series.

The Christmas novella, BEACH WALK ties in just before the third novel in the Emerald Isle, NC Stories Series (BEACH WEDDING).

BEACH WEDDING (Release Date 11/14/17) is the third novel in the Emerald Isle, NC Stories series.

Thank you for purchasing

BEACH WALK

I hope you enjoyed it!

Please leave a review where this book is sold. It helps authors find readers and helps readers find books they'll enjoy.

I hope you'll visit me at www.gracegreene.com and sign up for my newsletter. I'd love to be in contact with you.

Books by Grace Greene

Stories of heart and hope ~ from the Outer Banks to the Blue Ridge

Emerald Isle, NC Stories
Love. Suspense. Inspiration.

BEACH RENTAL (Emerald Isle novel #1)
BEACH WINDS (Emerald Isle novel #2)
BEACH WEDDING (Emerald Isle novel #3)
BEACH TOWEL (short story)
BEACH WALK (A Christmas novella)
BEACH CHRISTMAS (A Christmas novella)
CLAIR: BEACH BRIDES SERIES (novella)

Virginia Country Roads Novels
Love. Mystery. Suspense.

KINCAID'S HOPE
A STRANGER IN WYNNEDOWER
CUB CREEK (Cub Creek series #1)
LEAVING CUB CREEK (Cub Creek series #2)

Single Titles from Lake Union Publishing

THE HAPPINESS IN BETWEEN
THE MEMORY OF BUTTERFLIES

www.gracegreene.com

Made in the USA
Monee, IL
09 September 2020